ANNIE'S ATTIC MYSTERIES®

A Stony Point Christmas

K.D. McCrite

Annie's®

AnniesFiction.com

A Stony Point Christmas
Copyright © 2012, 2016 Annie's.

Library of Congress-in-Publication Data
A Stony Point Christmas / by K.D. McCrite
p. cm.
I. Title
                    2012946112

AnniesFiction.com
800-282-6643
Annie's Attic Mysteries®
Series Editors: Ken and Janice Tate
Series Creator: Stenhouse & Associates, Ridgefield, Connecticut

10 11 12 13 14 | Printed in China | 9 8 7 6 5

— Dedication —

Dedicated to Debbie Savannah George-Jones, who offered me friendship, fellowship, and a helping hand at a time when I needed it most.

1

The old man glowered at Annie Dawson from the other side of his campfire as she approached him. She'd been watching him for a while as she walked, noting how Maine's cold sea wind whipped his clothes and gray hair. Why would he be out on a morning in late November? And how could such a small fire possibly warm him?

"Hello," she said when she was close enough.

He stared at her from smoke- or wind-reddened eyes. Those eyes were as gray as the sea and the thin, snowy sky above it. His face, wrinkled and drawn, seemed to exude weariness.

"You need something?" he asked, his frown seemingly frozen in place.

"No, of course not."

Annie felt slightly baffled by his hostile attitude, and her first response was to take a step back. Having been born and raised in Texas, where folks were usually friendly, Annie never quite shook off her habit of greeting others with warmth. She was met with resistance to that habit when she'd first moved to Stony Point, Maine, a newcomer who tried too quickly and maybe too hard to fit in. By this time, though, Annie had learned to take things a little more slowly and let these New Englanders warm up to her. Still, it was hard to look at someone old, cold, and alone, and do nothing.

"No," she said again, reassuring him, "I want or need nothing except to make sure you're all right. Are you hungry? I'd be happy to fix you breakfast. You could warm up at my house, use the shower, if you'd like."

He stared hard at her.

"What makes you think I need anything you have to offer? And why should you care? You don't know me."

His harsh tone stung her worse than the cold wind.

"It's just so cold that I—"

"My welfare is no concern of yours." He turned his back and walked away from her.

Annie stood, the wind buffeting her. Her heart ached, not because of his sharp words, but because she knew he was more than cold and weary. His loneliness was almost a visible cloak around him. She wanted to go after him, but she didn't.

I suppose there are times, she thought, *when it's best not to follow your heart. And this seems to be one of them.*

She tightened the faux fur collar of her burgundy parka and tugged the crocheted ski hat more snugly over her head. Annie retraced her steps back to Grey Gables—the beautiful Victorian home bequeathed to her by her grandmother, Elizabeth Holden—wondering why she had chosen to walk along the beach on a snowy day in November, especially on a Tuesday before a Hook and Needle Club meeting. Actually—if she were honest with herself—Annie knew why, and perhaps on some level she had been hoping that the frigid temperature could chase out the pain she felt inside.

A week earlier her daughter LeeAnn had called. After the preliminary chitchat ended, Annie sensed LeeAnn had taken a deep, fortifying breath. It was the way LeeAnn had always prepared herself before engaging in serious conversation.

"Honey, what's wrong?" Annie had asked.

"Oh, Mom!" LeeAnn said, and Annie thought she heard tears in her daughter's voice.

"What is it? Tell me!"

"Mom, I'm so sorry." She broke off, and Annie heard the deep intake of breath again. A dozen scenarios ran through her mind all at once and so fast that she felt a little light-headed.

"LeeAnn, you're making me nervous."

"We can't come for Christmas!" LeeAnn blurted. "I'm so sorry. We just found out Herb's uncle is coming home for Christmas. He's the one who lives in Greenland, and it's been nearly fifteen years since he's been here. The visit is going to be really short, only three days, and ... well, Herb wants to be here and wants the kids and me to meet Uncle Bert, and really, it's the right thing to do. But—oh, Mom—I'm so sorry!"

Annie felt sick to her stomach with disappointment. She'd been looking forward to this Christmas for months.

"But I've made such plans!" she said before she could stop herself. Then, hearing the soft sound of LeeAnn's weeping, she tried to soothe her. "Oh, honey, please don't cry. Y'all can come visit later, it's all right." She put some brass to her voice. "In fact, having you visit in the winter is probably not a great idea anyway. You just never know what the weather is going to be, and travel can be so treacherous."

"Trust you to find the bright side," LeeAnn said,

sniffling. "But I *miss* you, Mom. So does Herb, and so do John and Joanna. They've been talking about seeing Grandma at Christmas for such a long time."

The last thing Annie wanted was for her daughter to feel worse than she obviously felt. She pushed herself to be as sunny as possible.

"Honey, it's all right. It's important to be with Herb's family while his uncle is there. Just think of all the tales he has about Greenland. It will be such fun for all of you and educational for the children. How many kids can say they know someone who lives in Greenland? Please don't worry about me. My goodness, I have more friends in Stony Point than I can count, and I have more things to do than I can accomplish in one lifetime, so I'll be just fine up here. I'll send everyone's gifts down, and you'll have a little part of me at Christmas anyway!"

LeeAnn sniffled some more, and Annie had to fight her own tears. She continued to reassure her daughter until, at last, LeeAnn accepted the situation with as much grace as possible. But after Annie hung up the telephone, the weight of this new development effectively doused most of her Christmas spirit.

Now, as she trudged back to Grey Gables, she tried to shove aside the scraps of her conversation with LeeAnn. Her encounter with the old man left Annie feeling even more deflated. Why had he been so rude when all she'd wanted was to be friendly?

Inside the house, she started to unwrap the layers of warm coverings she wore, but paused. The old man's coat, a lined denim jacket, was more suited to cutting wood on a cool fall day than a buffer between his body and the harsh northeast winter. His thin fisherman's hat had rested on his crown and didn't even reach his ears. He had no muffler around his neck and no thick gloves, only brown jersey ones. He was wearing shoes, not boots.

"Now, Annie, he doesn't want to be bothered," she said aloud. But the voice inside her heart spoke differently. It said, *Yes, he's cranky and rude, but he's also old and weary. He's alone and cold. He's probably hungry too.*

She glanced at her watch. The meeting would start in less than two hours. She still needed to shower and get dressed, and she had not even gathered up her crochet work to take along. She looked at the watch face again, counting ten tiny jerks of the second hand.

"I don't care what he said!" she declared to Boots, who sat yawning on the arm of the sofa. "I'll just have to be late for the meeting." The gray cat—also part of her grandmother's estate—simply blinked at her a moment, and then settled down, sphinxlike, and closed her eyes. Quite obviously Boots couldn't care less if Annie was late for the meeting, or if she missed it all.

Annie removed her gloves, scarf, and parka and then hurried to the kitchen. The room, with its soft yellow walls and white cabinets, always gave her comfort, and even on a cold winter's day, it seemed filled with sunshine and warmth. She made several sandwiches—ham and cheese, peanut butter and jelly, chicken salad—and put them in a basket. She added all the fruit she had in the house and a package of cookies. She made a thermos of coffee and tucked it into the basket. Upstairs she got a couple of blankets from the linen closet and pilfered through some of her crocheted items until she found a hat she was sure would fit him. A red-and-black-plaid mackinaw hung in the back of the closet in one of the spare rooms. Maybe it had belonged to her grandfather, Charles Holden, or maybe it was one of those items Gram had found and kept for whatever reason. Right then, its origins mattered nothing to Annie. It was a good, warm coat for a man.

Wrapped up once more against the cold weather, Annie rather awkwardly carried her collection of goods to the beach. She plowed against the wind and then followed the path she'd taken earlier. When she arrived at the campfire, the old man was gone, but a small fire still burned. She knew he was nearby, maybe even watching her.

"Hello!" she called. She expected no answer and got none. "Here is some food, some hot coffee, some blankets, and a coat."

She sat the items on the ground, but not too close to the fire where ashes or embers might present a danger. For a moment, Annie's gaze scoured the beach. She supposed she could follow his shoe prints and track him down like a fugitive, but doing so seemed intrusive, even invasive.

"I'm leaving now," she called again. After another few seconds, she walked away, slowly at first, giving him time to acknowledge her presence if he chose to do so, but at last, hurrying back to Grey Gables and the activities that the rest of the day held for her.

*   *   *   *

Annie was glad she hadn't gotten a speeding ticket, rushing to A Stitch in Time. She parked her faithful and much-loved Malibu a few doors down from the shop's front, and eyed the other cars already parked there. She recognized all the vehicles of the Hook and Needle Club membership.

"I am *so* late," she muttered, getting her plaid tote bag from the car. She fumbled and dropped her keys, and then she spilled some of the contents of her project bag onto the sidewalk. "Grrr!"

Annie glanced around to see if anyone in downtown Stony Point witnessed her less-than-graceful antics, and then she shoved everything back into the tote and hurried toward the shop.

The sound of voices and laughter met her before she opened the door. Once she stepped inside, the usual cordial warmth of the group seemed elevated. In fact, the meeting had more of a party atmosphere than a cozy craft circle. Annie glanced around the familiar shop, filled with its array of yarns, patterns, and other goods every crafter needed. No one noticed her late arrival. In fact, no one noticed her at all. Most of the women were standing, and all of them seemed to be talking at once. Their bright eyes and wide smiles told her something good was happening.

She put her project bag on the floor, peeled off her gloves, muffler, and coat, and then she removed her hat. Annie usually kept her pale blond hair in a simple short cut, but a new, very young hairdresser had given her a haircut a few days earlier, and Annie still wasn't used to it. There seemed to be too many short, choppy locks where she used to have longer, smooth strands. She tried to straighten, fluff, or smooth the "do" with her fingers. Thank goodness, hair grew back, and Annie planned never to allow Tiffany Wyman to touch her head again.

The meeting was so charged with gaiety, Annie smiled with anticipation as she hung up her coat and picked up her crochet work. She turned from the coatrack and noticed a stranger sitting next to dark-haired, outgoing Peggy Carson. Peggy, a waitress at The Cup & Saucer diner, chattered a mile a minute to Mary Beth Brock, the owner of A Stitch in Time.

The new member of the group had lank brown hair pulled back in a clasp at the nape of her neck, and she appeared thin, almost frail and rather young. She held her head bent over a tiny hook and quickly crocheted lace made of thin white thread. Something about that pale neck and small shoulders touched Annie. She settled down in the empty chair next to the woman.

"Hi," she said. "I'm Annie Dawson, and I'm another crocheter."

The woman lifted her head. She had lovely hazel eyes in a pale, careworn face. When she smiled shyly, the fine web of wrinkles deepened, giving her an illusion of age that may have been inaccurate.

Those eyes have seen a lot of pain, Annie thought.

"Hello." She put out her work-roughened right hand. "My name is Sara Downs." Her refined voice belied the impoverished appearance made by faded, loose-fitting clothes and mousy hair.

"Are you a newcomer to Stony Point?" Annie asked.

"Yes," she replied softly, turning back to her lace.

Annie waited a moment, but when the woman said nothing else, she asked, "Do you like it here?"

Sara nodded. "So far. Peggy has been very kind."

"Whoop!" Peggy said, turning in her seat. "I heard my name. Oh, Annie! I didn't see you come in. Have you met Sara?" With short, dark curly hair and a rather round face, the slightly chubby Peggy always gave off an air of friendliness and enthusiasm. Her eyes sparkled as she smiled at the two women.

"Hi, Peggy," Annie said. "Yes, we just now met. She was telling me you've been very kind." Annie shifted a look back and forth between the two women. "Are you related, cousins or something?"

"Nothing like that!" Peggy sang out, patting Sara's arm. "Sara started working in the kitchen at The Cup & Saucer. The other day on our break, she told me she loves to crochet, so I invited her to visit our little group. Maybe the Hook and Needle Club will get a new member." She beamed at Sara, who smiled shyly and kept crocheting.

"We always need new blood," Annie declared with a light laugh. "Maybe you can tell us some interesting new tales while we work. We've all heard one another's stories so many times, nothing is new anymore."

"Oh, my," Sara said, lifting her head quickly. She looked a little like a cornered animal. "I have no stories to tell. I'm dull as toast, actually."

"Oh, Sara, I bet you'll have plenty to say, once you warm up to us," Peggy said with a laugh. She looked at Annie. "Have you heard the news?"

"News? You mean whatever it is that has everyone in here chattering like a bunch of magpies? Apparently not. What's going on?"

The news must be significant for no one to have noticed this awful haircut, Annie thought. *Thank goodness for that.*

"It seems that Norma—"

"Annie!" Alice shrieked from across the room. She ran up to the small circle that now surrounded Annie. "Isn't it fantastic, Annie?"

Alice MacFarlane, with flashing blue eyes and rich, shoulder-length auburn hair, was Annie's best friend and closest neighbor.

Before Annie could respond, Peggy looked at Alice and said just a little testily, "I'm trying to tell her right now."

The two friends eyed each other as if they might have a spat over who got to reveal the news to Annie. She never liked it when her friends fussed at each other.

"Maybe I'll just ask Kate," Annie said, starting to rise.

"Norma got some money!" Peggy blurted.

"Norma at the post office?"

"Yes!" Alice said. "She got to work this morning and there was an envelope in the outgoing mail basket with her name printed across it, no address or anything. When she opened it, guess what?"

"Twenty one-hundred dollar bills," Peggy said. "Two thousand dollars, *cash!*"

"My stars!" Annie said.

"And that's not all—" Alice said.

"Grace Hitchens had a note stuck to her front door that said her hospital bill had been paid in full!" Peggy said. "There was a note in the envelope with Norma's money too."

Annie's mouth fell open. Grace Hitchens had been hospitalized for nearly five months. Her house was on the market, and she'd already sold her car. No one had known what would happen to her if the house sold because she had no family to rely on. In fact, the Hook and Needle Club had talked about organizing some kind of fundraising for her. And Norma, a single woman working only part-time now and facing retirement soon, was often on Annie's mind.

"That's absolutely wonderful!" she said. "Who did such a lovely, generous thing?"

Mary Beth joined the group. Stocky-built with salt-and-pepper hair, she was the one who welcomed new members to the Hook and Needle Club with open arms and kept the group organized.

"That's what has everyone so mystified, Annie," she said. "No one knows!"

"There wasn't a name or anything?"

"There was a *name*, but we don't know who it's really from." Mary Beth's voice carried such authority that neither Alice nor Peggy said a word.

"What did the notes say?" Annie asked Mary Beth.

"They were exactly the same. They read, 'An early Merry Christmas, from Santa Claus.'"

"Nothing more than *that*?" Annie asked.

"That's it," Mary Beth said. "Odd, isn't it?"

"Looks like Santa exists in Stony Point, even if you can't find him anywhere else," Sara murmured.

Annie glanced at her, wondering what unhappy events in this woman's past caused her to say that.

"What fun it must be to receive an anonymous gift!" dark-haired Kate Stevens said as she joined the group. "And how great for Norma and Mrs. Hitchens. I wonder if anyone else in town got money or had a bill paid."

"We'll hear about it, if it's so," Mary Beth said.

"Well, I think it's a grand thing to help others, but it's foolish to do so anonymously. It makes poor business sense!" This comment came from the stern, elderly, well-to-do Stella Brickson, who, until one got to know her, often seemed to have either no heart or a very cold one. By now, however, Annie realized that the white-haired woman's gruffness was nothing more than a rough exterior to shield her from hurt. Annie was glad she'd finally broken through that barrier to discover the good woman beneath Stella's hard polish.

"Oh, but you can't always measure the worth of things by how much sense they make or how well they benefit business," Kate said.

"That's right," said Gwendolyn Palmer as she settled into her chair. If anyone would know the flash and benefit of business, it would be the classically beautiful and perfectly groomed Gwen. She and her banker husband, John, lived on the same hill as Annie's Grey Gables in a lovely colonial home called Wedgwood. Pillars of the community, she and John were well-liked by everyone. Gwen extracted knitting needles and tawny-colored yarn from her sleek bag. "I say God bless this person, whoever he or she is!"

"Well, of course!" Stella sniffed. "I didn't mean to imply that one should not give unless it's a tax write-off."

"Of course you didn't, Stella," Annie said. "We know that, don't we, ladies?"

A chorus of agreement passed through the group.

"It's a generous and beautiful thing for someone to do," Alice said, "but altruism aside, I want to know who it is!"

"Well, don't we all?" Peggy said. She met Annie's eyes and added, "Annie! You're our sleuth-in-residence. Why don't you investigate? You lead; we'll follow!"

Annie's mouth dropped open for a second time.

"Now, Peggy, I—"

"I think that's a great idea," Alice said.

Kate smiled and said, "Me too."

The other women nodded, and a general "Yes-do-it!" air hung in the room.

Annie put down the silvery-gray crocodile-stitch shawl she had started two days earlier. She'd thought all her Christmas gifts had been made, but since her family would not be coming to Maine for the holiday, she wanted to add a few more gifts to the ones she was sending. She had made John and Joanna each a pair of colorful toe-socks, crocheted Herb a pair of house slippers, and this shawl would be elegant enough that LeeAnn could wear it when she and Herb went out on the town.

Annie now looked around the room, passing a glance across each smiling, eager face that turned toward her.

"Ladies, I hate to throw cold water on your idea, but if whoever gave Norma money or paid off Mrs. Hitchens's hospital bill wanted you to know his or her identity, you would already know it."

A dead silence fell, and then Alice finally broke it. "Just because you don't have the Christmas spirit yet, Annie Dawson, there's no reason to sour it for everyone else."

"This has nothing whatsoever to do with Christmas spirit," Annie protested. "But y'all seem to want me to try to discover who this ... this ... secret Santa is, and I'm not going to do it!"

"And you shouldn't!" Mary Beth said. She gave a little laugh. "Ladies, we've spent nearly half our meeting time chattering about Grace Hitchens and Norma. Let's turn our attention to other matters. If you want to bring any Christmas goodies to the meetings to share, be aware that my old refrigerator is on the blink. In fact, it died a few days ago, and so did my egg salad. So bring nonperishable snacks. And now, we need to discuss this year's Christmas project."

The Hook and Needle Club members had been asked to create a quilt of squares depicting the town's landmarks. It was to be displayed at a New Year's Day celebration at the Town Hall.

"Oh, goodness gracious!" Annie muttered in aggravation as she searched in vain in her tote. "I meant to work on mine while I was here, but I left it at home. "

"I have my squares finished!" Stella said, putting aside the dark blue glove she was knitting.

"Good, Stella," Mary Beth said. "I finished mine just last night." She held up a square with the embroidered image of A Stitch in Time in winter.

"That's lovely!" Gwen said.

"Mary Beth, it looks like a picture!" said Peggy.

"Thank you. Now, ladies, I realize the holiday rush is upon us," Mary Beth said somewhat breathlessly, as if the very idea of getting the quilt finished pressured her, "but if you can get your squares to me as soon as possible ..." She gave them an encouraging smile that seemed to have an edge of panic in it. "I realize most of us would rather have an old-fashioned quilting bee to put it together like we had a few years go, and I agree it would be fun, but in the interest of time I've contacted Barb Westinghouse. Her quilting machine is the absolute best, and she promises to get our project fully quilted in good time, *if* we can get all the blocks to her no later than a week from Wednesday." She paused. "You will do that, won't you?"

"I wish I could participate," Sara whispered to Annie, "but I haven't been here long enough to know a landmark when I see one."

Annie's heart warmed as she and the shy Sara shared a smile.

"That's OK," she whispered back. "There are plenty of Hook and Needle Club projects coming up."

"Good! I'd love to help." She ducked her head and busily worked on her bit of lace.

"My squares don't look so good, but I'm nearly finished," Kate said. She gazed at Stella and sighed. "I wish I had your quilting experience. Your squares are so lovely."

"Do you have your squares with you, Stella?" Annie asked.

"I have both of them." She reached into her basket and

drew out a lovely square that depicted the new Historical Society building, complete with the sign in the front that read "Stony Point Historical Society." The other square she had made pictured the new Cultural Center. The ladies expressed their approval and examined Stella's precise workmanship as she passed the squares around to each member.

"What is yours?" Sara asked as Annie passed the squares to Alice on the other side of her.

"Grey Gables, of course," she replied with a smile and then realized Sara wouldn't know about Grey Gables. "It's the home I inherited from my grandmother—an old Victorian house on Ocean Drive. It has a great big porch and lots of windows, and in the summer there are so many flowers!"

"Sounds lovely!" Sara sighed. She glanced at her watch, sliding her crocheting into a battered oversized black purse. "I promised to be back at work by noon. Excuse me, please." She stood and then passed a quick gaze around to everyone. "It was lovely to meet all of you."

She left so quickly and quietly, it was almost as if she hadn't been there at all.

"What an odd little woman," Stella said. Her knitting needles clicked swiftly as she resumed work on the glove. "I don't believe she said two words until the moment she took her leave." She shot a sharp glance at Peggy. "She came with you, didn't she, Peggy? Where on earth did you find her? She's not a relative—is she?"

Several of the women shifted restlessly as Stella spoke. Annie wondered if they were as uncomfortable as she was with Stella's somewhat haughty tone.

"She started working at The Cup & Saucer a few days ago," Peggy said, preparing to return to the diner herself. "She just seemed so ... oh, I don't know ... sort of ... well, in need of friends, I guess." She looked at each woman. "I thought the Hook and Needle Club would be a good place for her to meet some nice people."

There was the briefest silence then Mary Beth said, "Of course it is! I hope she comes back."

"Me too," Annie said, stoutly.

"So do I," said Gwen. "Don't you Stella?"

Stella knitted with renewed industry, blushing just a bit. "Of course."

*   *   *   *

The uproar caused by Grace Hitchens's and Norma's gifts had so consumed thoughts and conversation at the meeting that it wasn't until after she went home that Annie remembered her encounter with the strange old man on the beach. She had meant to mention him to her friends to find out if any of them had seen him or knew who he was.

She stood at her front door, key in hand, staring toward the restless ocean. Had he found her gifts? Did he make use of them? Should she see if he needed anything else? She pondered the wisdom of going to check on him. A little nudge from her brain encouraged her to leave him alone, but her soft heart could not dismiss him so easily.

Upstairs, she changed into warmer clothes once again and hesitated only a moment at the edge of the veranda before retracing her steps down the path and along the beach to his campfire. By the time she reached the site, nothing remained but a bit of charred wood, now cold and damp from dousing. The moist sand and dirt around the campfire showed signs of having been disturbed, but she saw no footprints leading away in any direction except her own.

Annie breathed in the pungent aroma of damp ash and seaside. She sighed heavily, staring along the rocky shore in one direction and then the other as far as she could see. She turned and allowed her eyes to scour every nook, tree, or hillock, and saw nothing. At last, sighing again, she trudged back to Grey Gables.

At least the food, the coat, and the blankets were gone. She took some comfort in that.

∼ 2 ∼

Annie knocked on Ian Butler's door promptly at seven o'clock Friday evening. A few moments later the mayor of Stony Point opened his front door.

"Hi, Annie!" he exclaimed, greeting her with a huge smile. "Come in out of the cold."

Handsome and refined, with graying hair, Ian wore jeans and a dark green flannel shirt. She entered his warm house and admired the spotless simplicity of it. Cream-color walls and white trim contrasted nicely with the polished dark-walnut floors.

"I brought popcorn!" she said, holding up a large bag of unpopped buttered kernels for the microwave.

"And I have cider and a movie!" he replied, taking her coat. He eyed her black slacks and pearl-gray sweater appreciatively. "You look lovely, Annie. I like your hair fixed like that. Come into the den and have a seat. Would you like a mug of hot cider?"

"I'd love it," she said, handing him the popcorn and touching her hair with tentative fingers. Did he really like the style, or was he just saying that because he was nice?

He looked at box and laughed. "Ah! Double butter! My favorite."

"Mine too."

He led her into the den with his schnauzer, Tartan, trailing them.

"Have a seat, Annie; I'll be right back."

Rather than follow Ian out of the room, Tartan chose to reacquaint himself with Annie. He sniffed her shoes and her slacks, leaving a trail of silver dog hair where he touched her clothing. He seemed especially interested in the right sleeve of her sweater, and no wonder. Annie had picked up Boots right before she left Grey Gables to tell her, "Be a good kitty while I'm gone."

Finally, Tartan raised his brown eyes to Annie's face, cocked his head to one side, and wagged his stumpy tail.

"Ah—so now you've decided you approve of me, do you?" she asked with a laugh, rubbing the dog's soft ears. Tartan seemed to smile at her and settled on the floor near her feet.

The den was a lovely, cozy place to enjoy an evening. A fire burned in the fireplace and lent a soft glow to old-fashioned, golden knotty-pine walls and the soft, brown carpet. The overstuffed furniture with dark brown chenille upholstery and wide arms fit the comfortable atmosphere. The polished surfaces of the pine coffee table and matching end tables gleamed in the soft lamplight and glow of the fireplace. On either side of the fireplace, bookshelves nearly overflowed with books that were both lined up on end and stacked on their sides. On the mantel, Ian displayed several framed photographs, mostly of him and his late wife, Arianna. A couple of the photos were of Tartan looking every inch the beloved dog he was. The walls boasted mostly prints or photographs of various lighthouses and clipper ships. All in all, the room exuded comfort and masculinity.

From his place on the floor, Tartan rested his chin on his paw and sighed with contentment. Annie reached down and patted him.

"You're a special fellow, aren't you, boy?" she asked.

"That pooch loves attention!" Ian said as he returned. He handed Annie a cup of hot cider embellished with a cinnamon stick and settled near her on the sofa.

"He's a sweet dog," she said, continuing to rub Tartan's head. "Some days I think Boots would be content to sit in my lap all day long. Of course, when I'm sitting, I'm usually crocheting, and Boots wreaks havoc with that."

"I can imagine." He leaned down to scratch Tartan behind one ear. The little tail wriggled with delight. Ian straightened, laughing. "I'm a sap for that little guy, but don't tell anyone. So, how was the Hook and Needle Club meeting Tuesday? Are the quilt blocks finished?"

"Most of them. Mary Beth has been doing her best to muscle us into action!"

"Yeah," he said, eyes twinkling, "she's such a battle-ax."

"For shame, Ian Butler!" Annie let her eyes twinkle back, knowing he was just teasing. He and Mary Beth were great friends.

"I'm such a brute."

"You truly are."

They laughed. Tartan jumped up on the sofa, wedging himself between them.

"He wants to get in on the fun," Annie said, shifting her body to make room for the dog.

"Well, on these cold nights, he likes to snuggle up. It's good to have a warm friend, isn't it, Tartan?"

For a brief moment, Annie's thoughts went to the old man on the beach, wondering where he slept, and if he was warm enough. She started to mention him, but an inexplicable something counseled her to say nothing right then.

"What do you think about those anonymous good deeds for Grace Hitchens and Norma?" Ian asked.

"I think giving anonymous gifts is a grand idea!" Annie exclaimed.

He sipped his cider and then set his mug on the coffee table. He had an almost smug smile on his face. Annie narrowed her eyes, studying him as he wiped a drop from the shining table. Maybe in some enigmatic way, he was telling her he knew more than he let on.

"What about you, Ian?" she asked, head cocked to one side.

He sat back and raised one eyebrow. "What about me?"

"What do you think about those 'mysterious' gifts?"

"I can't think of anyone I'd rather see receive help more than those two women."

"I completely agree," she said, twisting her mouth in thought, contemplating the possibility of Ian Butler handing out gifts without identifying himself. It was something he would do.

"Annie?" Ian said after a brief pause. "I see an odd look on your face. What's going on?"

"Odd look?" She straightened her shoulders, smoothed her hair, and brushed any invisible dust or wrinkles from her clothes. "What's odd?"

"I didn't say *you* looked odd. You just have a … an expression on your face, as if you have a secret."

Her mouth flew open in surprise. "A secret?" she asked. "Me? What secret would I have?"

His sly grin confused her. Then she thought about the old man and wondered if Ian knew about him, but when he spoke again she saw his mind had gone in another direction entirely.

"You seem to know more about the mysterious Santa than you're sharing."

She frowned, and shook her head. "I don't know anything about it," Annie said. "But you, Ian Butler, are smiling like the cat that swallowed the canary."

He lifted both brows and laughed heartily. "That's a phrase I haven't heard in a long time," he said. "But if I'm acting like that cat, I certainly do so without realizing it."

They stared at each other, suspicion mirrored in their eyes. Ian shook his head and looked away, reaching for his drink.

"It seems like every phone call I get and everyone I see in the office or in town wants to know who gave Norma money and who paid off Grace's medical bills. It seems I can't get away from wondering about it. How about you, Annie?"

"I've not given it a lot of thought, actually. I've been really busy working on Christmas gifts. Plus, I'm putting the finishing touches on my quilt square before Mary Beth has a stroke."

"That quilt will be great," Ian said. "She told me what everyone is doing, and it's going to be so nice. But, seriously, with your penchant for investigating mysteries, you haven't ferreted out the identity of our secret Santa?"

"No. As I told the others on Tuesday, if the person wants to keep his or her identity a secret, then we shouldn't go snooping."

Ian gave her a look of extreme skepticism, but what he said was, "Whatever you say, Annie."

She had a sudden flash of insight which made her gasp and sit back, nearly spilling her cider. "You don't think … surely, Ian, you don't for a minute think the secret Santa is me!"

He shrugged. "It's something you would do, Annie. And I'm not the only one who thinks so."

This time she did spill a little cider, as her muscles went slack from surprise. She fumbled and tightened her grip.

"Oh, I'm so sorry!" She madly brushed droplets from the sofa. "You mean …?"

He grinned.

"Yep! Stony Point suspects you," he said.

Pure silence filled the room for a moment before Annie set down her mug.

"It's ridiculous, of course. Not that I wouldn't love to be such a generous donor of gifts, but I don't have that kind of money. Why, Grace Hitchens's hospital bill alone must have been astronomical, and that doesn't include doctor bills and the cost of her medicines."

She watched as the logic in her statement settled into Ian's mind. The speculative look faded from his eyes.

"Of course," he said quietly, smiling. "It's just that you're such a beloved person in town, and you're Betsy Holden's granddaughter, and well, people put two and two together and came up with seven."

"Helping someone in trouble *was* Gram's way," Annie replied. "And I'm flattered that you—and others—thought I could make such a gesture. But, please, Ian, the next time someone suggests me, tell them the truth."

He reached over, clasped her hand warmly and squeezed it. "I'll tell them. But it *is* something you'd do."

She returned his smile, but before the intimate moment and warm touch could turn into something more, she withdrew her hand from his and glanced at the three DVD cases on the coffee table.

"Which one are we watching tonight?" she said merrily, picking up the stack. "Ah, classics—*Casablanca* and *The Quiet Man*—and one new one—*The Help*."

"I tell you what, Annie," he said as he got up. He picked up the popcorn. "I'll go fix our snacks, and you choose the show." He gave her wink as if they were in a conspiracy of some sort.

Annie wanted to stand by her declaration not to unravel this mystery, but if people in Stony Point bandied about her name, giving her credit for something she had not done, she had to put a stop to that. Others might expect her to do more, to give what she did not have. A myriad of disastrous scenarios burst in her mind's eyes. Perhaps it would be best, after all, if she found out the identity of Stony Point's Santa.

— 3 —

On Saturday morning, Annie woke up just before daybreak to the sound of howling wind. By this time, she'd lived in Stony Point long enough to know that wind buffeting her house like that often brought a ton of snow with it. The sound made her shiver, and she snuggled down in her warm nest of blankets. At some point in the night Boots had nosed her way beneath the covers and was now curled up, sound asleep, warm and furry next to Annie's stomach.

Annie smiled and stroked the cat's soft coat gently. She felt herself drifting back into the safety net of sleep, away from the sound of that wind and the frigid air. If she were to get out of bed and turn up the thermostat, the house would be warm by the time she was ready to get up for the day. Instead, she cuddled further against the soft pillow beneath her head and the warm cat by her tummy.

Uninvited, a vision edged its way into her mind and consciousness. The old man, his thin coat, his small cap, those ridiculous jersey gloves … she imagined him shivering, hunched over from cold, weak from hunger.

Annie sat straight up. The blankets fell away, Boots woke up, and cool air whooshed around her. She was wide awake now, and she all but jumped out of bed. Rubbing her arms and shivering, she hurried to the thermostat, turning it up several degrees. She grabbed her robe, thrust feet into slippers and went downstairs to make fresh coffee. She did not cast a passing glance out the window because she knew what she'd see out there: early morning darkness made even darker by the dreary winter day.

Why'd I ever leave Texas? she asked herself as she scurried back upstairs to get dressed. Of course she realized early December anywhere north of the Mason-Dixon Line was not exactly balmy. But still … a girl could dream of Texas bluebonnets and warm breezes.

When Annie left the house a bit later, the first signs of gray daylight barely seeped through the clouds. Clutched tightly against her chest was a large thermos of hot coffee. She had bundled herself thickly against the cold. She thought of the movie *A Christmas Story* and the little boy who, once he fell, could not get up again because of his winter wraps and had lain in the snow like a bug on its back. She hoped she stayed upright.

Her eyes watered so much in the wind she could hardly see. Only the notion of saving someone from freezing to death propelled her forward. She prayed she wasn't too late, but feared she probably was. Blinking hard, she looked ahead and thought she saw a movement. She wiped her eyes and cupped her hands on either side of her face to block the wind.

It was he. She was sure of it, and she rushed on, fighting the freezing gust that tried to shove her back. The more the wind pushed, the harder she pressed forward. Once again she cupped her eyes and peered ahead. He turned and disappeared into a rocky cove. Had he seen her? She could not be sure, and even if he had retreated from her approach, she did not stop or slow. She rounded the large rocky out-cropping and caught sight of him several yards away. In that cove, the wind seemed less aggressive, and she walked on without such struggle.

"Hello, there!" she shouted, hoping he heard her above the sound of the wind and surf. Maybe he did not hear, or maybe he chose not to hear. In either case, she refused to ignore the urge to check on his welfare.

She followed his tracks and found, far back behind the big rocks, a tiny shack nearly hidden in the trees, well-protected from the wind. The smoke from his chimney disappeared as quickly as it rose.

The old man stood on the little stoop in front of his door, glowering at her, arms folded across his chest.

"Good morning!" she called with more friendly cheer than she felt. She wondered if her frozen cheeks would crack from the broad smile she offered him.

He said nothing as she approached, but the expression in his gray eyes blazed with resistance.

"I don't want callers," he said when she was close enough to hear him, "especially those who feel the need to come calling on me unawares in early morning hours." His glare deepened. "I don't like people of the snoopy sort."

Had the weather been warmer, Annie's smile likely would have melted from her face. As it was, it seemed fro-zen in place, aching against her teeth and cheekbones.

"I apologize for inconveniencing you," she said, "but not for checking on your well-being—"

"No one asked you to!"

"I know that. But, sir, you aren't ... you aren't a young man. And the other day when I saw you, your clothing seemed inadequate ..." He did not so much as blink. "I wanted to be sure you had food and warmth ... you did get my bundle, didn't you?"

There seemed to be a twitch in his right cheek.

"Yes."

Annie did not expect a "thank you," and she didn't receive one. She held his gaze and thought she saw, beneath his surly demeanor, a wisp of embarrassment. If her offering embarrassed him, she regretted he felt that way. Nevertheless, she had no intention of leaving his presence until she was sure he would survive bad weather.

"Are you a native of this part of the world?" she asked.

"I fail to see why that's any business of yours," he said. "Now, kindly leave my property."

She stayed put.

"The only reason I asked is because Maine winters, especially right here so close to the coastline, can be brutal. I'm from Texas, and it took me a while—"

"I understand cold weather and the pitfalls of living near northern waters. I'm considerably older, and I daresay, much smarter than you."

Annie folded her arms in an exact replica of his stance.

"Sir, I came to you with good intentions. I have offered you nothing but kindness. I refuse to leave until I'm sure you have sufficient shelter, water, and food."

He said nothing for a moment and then took a deep breath.

"So be it. I have plenty of everything I need. Good day to you, ma'am."

With that, he turned and went into the shack. He shut the door firmly, and Annie heard the distinct, finalizing click of a lock. She straightened her shoulders even more, went to the door and shouted into the keyhole, "I'm going to check on you from time to time."

She waited a short time, but he never responded. She turned on her heel and hurried back to Grey Gables the way she'd come, fighting the wind and squinting against frozen moisture now pelting her face.

Back home, Annie's cold-stiffened fingers could barely unlock her front door. It seemed to her that her flannel-lined, down-stuffed, sturdy leather gloves should have provided more comfort than they did.

Inside the house, the warmth greeted her with as much love as she greeted it. She was met with silence and glanced around for Boots, who generally showed up to blink at her, either in greeting, entreating, or accusation. Had the cat slipped outside while Annie maneuvered her bulky self through the door earlier? Her heart nearly stopped at the idea.

"Boots?" Her voice came out weak, half-frozen. She cleared her throat, coughed hard, and cleared her throat again. "Boots?" she called somewhat frantically.

She heard, very faintly, a tiny, high sound like "Mmm?"

"Where are you, kitty?" She followed the sound, and found Boots emerging from sleep, half-burrowed into a soft rose-pink afghan in the corner of the sofa. The cat mewed softly again, blinked sleepily, and then yawned.

"I'm sorry I woke you," Annie said with a laugh.

Boots leaped to the floor and strolled toward Annie, tail

high, eyes bright. She meowed plaintively, gave Annie's legs a quick rub of her arched body and then circled, meowing her demand.

"Hungry. I know. Let's get you fed."

She picked up the cat, loving the soft, purring warmth against her cold palms and fingers. As soon as she fed Boots and gave her fresh water, Annie took a long shower. The water was so hot that steam filled the room and fogged the shower doors and mirror. It seemed she'd never get warm, but eventually the core of her body felt comfortable again. She dressed in dark gray fleece slacks and heavy wool sweater only a couple of shades lighter than black. Thick gray kneesocks and stylish black leather boots finished that day's garb.

Annie had just finished blow-drying her hair when she heard someone at the door. She glanced out the window. This was the kind of snow that iced over roadways and sidewalks, and made travel dangerous. Who in the world would come out on day this raw? Had the old man come to her, after all, seeking the secure shelter of Grey Gables?

She hurried downstairs and to the front door.

"Annie!" Alice said as Annie turned the knob. "It's so c-cold! May I come in?"

"Come in!" Annie said, tugging her friend's snowy arm. "What on earth are you doing out in this weather? Want some hot coffee?" She shut the door.

"I wanted to visit, and yes, I'll take hot coffee. Gladly."

They went to the kitchen together. Annie supposed there would never be a time in her life that she did not feel the welcome of this kitchen every time she entered it. The room seemed to embody the presence of Gram in every corner and cupboard. How many times in this same kitchen had Annie and Alice shared snacks that Gram had prepared in the summers of their youth? Annie's annual visits while her parents were overseas on their mission work had cemented a friendship that bloomed again after Betsy Holden's death and Annie's return to Stony Point.

"I brought cinnamon rolls," Alice said, pulling a container from beneath her bulky coat, "with orange zest icing and pecans."

"Lovely!" Annie said. "I'm starved."

Alice gave her a long hard stare as she unbuttoned her coat and hung it on a hook near the back door.

"You are extremely frazzled for this early in the morning." She glanced at the clock. "It's barely 8 a.m., but you look like you've already been on a shopping trip to Portland. What's up?"

Annie gave her a wide-eyed look, wondering how Alice MacFarlane always seemed to read her like a book.

"You aren't trying to uncover the identity of our Stony Point Santa, are you?" Alice asked before Annie opened her mouth.

"No, I've not done that at all." She paused. "Yet."

"Ah ha!" Alice smiled. "I knew you wouldn't be able to leave it alone. You're a mystery magnet."

"It's not that," Annie said, slightly frowning. She turned and measured water for the coffeemaker.

"But aren't you curious?"

"Of course I'm curious," Annie said over her shoulder, scooping fresh coffee grounds into the maker.

"I sense a 'but' in there."

"*But* ...," Annie said as switched on the coffeemaker, "Ian says some people in town think *I* am the person who did it." When Alice did not respond, Annie said, "You don't think that, do you, Alice?"

"Well, to be honest ...."

"Oh, come on! Where would I get that kind of money?"

Alice shrugged. "I don't know. But it's something you'd do, Annie."

"That's what Ian said Friday night," Annie replied, sounding somewhat fretful, even to her own ears. "He said Gram would have done it, and I'm a lot like her."

"True."

"Oh for goodness' sake!" She sat down heavily. "That's why I need to discover who the giver is, so no one credits me for giving Norma a hunk of money and freeing Grace from that enormous hospital bill."

"And buying Bud Favor a new motorcycle."

Annie gawked at her. "Buying Bud Favor a new motorcycle?" Bud Favor was a hardworking college student who commuted daily to Portland on an old motorcycle that seemed held together with twine and duct tape.

"It was on his porch last night about nine o'clock. It had a big red bow and a note signed 'Early Merry Christmas, from Stony Point's Santa.'"

"That's wonderful!" Annie said, smiling. "Now his mother can stop worrying so much about him getting to school and back. Though in the winter, travel on a motorcycle can be harsh. Especially in weather like this."

Her mind drifted to the old man again. Was he warm and dry? Did he need fuel?

"Oh, my. What's that?" Alice said.

Annie glanced around, a little alarmed. "What's what? Where? Is something wrong?"

"That look on your face. It's the same frazzled look you had when you opened the front door."

Annie leaned back. "Oh."

"Oh."

She met Alice's eyes. "There's this man—"

"A man?" Alice echoed with excitement. She leaned forward, eyes bright. "Who is it? Do I know him? Does he live here? Where'd you meet him? Why haven't you told me about him before now? *What about Ian?*"

In spite of herself and the situation, Annie laughed. She answered Alice's questions in the order they were asked.

"I don't know his name. I don't know him. He lives in a shack. I met him on the beach. And I didn't want to tell anyone about him because he's … well, he guards his privacy. And what about Ian?" She got up to pour their coffee. "You want to put the rolls in the microwave to warm them? They smell heavenly, by the way."

"Annie Dawson!" Alice said after a moment of gawking at her friend. She made no move to unwrap her rolls and heat them. "Have you lost your mind? That guy sounds like a wacko. He guards his privacy? What does that mean? Is he an escaped convict or something?"

"I don't know who he is," Annie said again, "but I doubt there is anything to be afraid of. He's quite old."

"Well, yeah, so is Charles Manson. Did this guy have wild eyes like Charles Manson?"

"Oh, *Alice!*" Annie all but shrieked. "That poor old

man is *not* Charles Manson. He's just an old derelict living in a terrible old shack down the beach a ways, back in a cove."

Alice heaved out a huge breath.

"How in the world did you unearth someone living in a shack on the beach in December in Maine?"

"You make it sound like I dug him up out of a grave or something. I didn't 'unearth' him."

Alice just shrugged and kept the waiting, skeptical expression on her face.

"I saw him the other day," Annie continued. "He was hunched over a campfire and dressed in clothes that really were unsuitable for the weather."

Alice propped her elbows on the table and cupped her chin as Annie related the details of both of her encounters with the old man.

"I'm just so worried about him, Alice," she concluded. "What if he starves or freezes?"

"Annie, you've taken him clothes, food, and blankets. What more can you do? I wonder who he is?"

Annie shook her head. "I wish I knew. If I knew his name, maybe I could find his family and see if they'd come and get him. He ought to be in a warm house, not that old shack. You know it must be cold in there all the time, Alice, so close to the water."

"Did he seem like his mind was clear? Maybe he has dementia or something."

"No, I'm sure he's in complete control of his faculties," Annie said. "I mean, he seemed eccentric, yes, but not out of his mind. His eyes were clear—angry, but clear."

Alice frowned as she got up and began unwrapping the rolls.

"Honestly, Annie, who do you know that's in full control of their faculties that would live in a shack on the beach up here in the winter?"

"You have a point." Annie sighed. "On the other hand, maybe he doesn't care that it's cold and he's miserable. Maybe he *isn't* cold and miserable. Maybe he's lived as a transient all his life, and he's used to hardship and can take it."

Alice arranged the thick, soft cinnamon rolls on a plate and put them in the microwave. She set the timer and pushed the button.

"You think he's a transient?" she asked, licking a drop of icing from her fingertip.

Annie shrugged.

"If so," Alice continued, "you're right in saying he's used to hardship and making do. Maybe he prefers it."

"From his anger and resistance to my help, I'd say he definitely prefers it."

The microwave timer dinged. Alice opened the door and the aroma of hot cinnamon and tangy orange filled the kitchen.

"Annie, my friend," she said as she carefully removed the plate, "your heart is as soft and gooey as the center of these rolls, and your personality is as sweet as this icing, but this time I think you are probably wasting your good intentions. The man has survived this long without your help; I have no doubt he wants it to stay that way."

"I'm sure you're right," Annie said. "I should just put him out of my mind."

"Yes."

"Just forget all about him."

"Yes."

"Don't give him another moment's thought."

"That's my suggestion," Alice agreed.

Alice sat down a small plate in front of Annie with a huge, warm roll covering most of the surface. Considering that she'd risen early, walked far, returned disheartened, all on an empty stomach, Annie was sure she could devour not only this roll but the other three Alice had brought with her as well.

She stared down at the creamy white icing that oozed into the crevices of the roll. The fragrance of yeast, cinnamon, sugar, and orange rose to coax her appetite into full throttle.

"I still plan to check on him often and make sure he's all right," she said as she sank her fork into the tender pastry.

"I guess I should just change the subject," Alice said.

"I would." Annie put the forkful of cinnamon roll into her mouth and smiled at her friend.

"OK," Alice said, smiling back. "So what were you and Ian doing Friday night?"

— 4 —

"*H*ow did your Princessa jewelry meeting go last night?" Annie asked, putting off her best friend's prying question about her movie night with Ian.

"Lovely," Alice said. "There's a beautiful new line of rose gold coming out soon. You might like to see the previews of what they're going to offer. I don't have any samples yet." She got up to fish a catalog out of her coat pocket. She handed it to Annie. "But you're avoiding my question. How'd your date go with Ian?"

"It wasn't a date. I just went over there for popcorn and a movie. These are beautiful, Alice. I want to see some of them when you get your samples."

Alice gave her a sharp look, but then dropped the subject of Ian Butler.

"By the way, Annie, did you get to talk much to the new woman at the Hook and Needle Club last week?" She sat down.

"You mean Sara Downs? We talked for a bit, but she seems rather shy."

"I noticed that," Alice said. "Do you know anything about her?"

"Not really. Probably less than you do."

"Why less than me?" Alice asked.

"Because," Annie said, pointing the tines of her

fork at Alice, "you have a way of extracting information from people."

Alice rolled her eyes. "I'm merely curious, that's all. You, on the other hand, are the true detective."

"Be that as it may," Annie said as she got up to rinse off her sticky plate, "I'm not probing into her life just to satisfy your curiosity. And by the way, that was the best cinnamon roll I've ever had in my life."

"Thanks. So do you know where Sara came from?" Alice asked.

"She didn't tell me."

"Hmm," Alice mused. "Do you know how old she is?"

"No."

Alice twisted her mouth. "Is she married?"

"I don't know," Annie said. "Give me your plate, and I'll rinse it off."

Alice handed it over absentmindedly. "I wonder if she has kids."

Annie put the dishes in the dishwasher and closed it. She turned to her friend.

"Alice, my dear, if you are so all-fired curious about the woman, then ask her all these questions at the next meeting."

Alice pulled in the corners of her mouth. "All right. I will!"

"Good. Now, come into the living room. I finished Ian's sweater the other day, and I want you to see it."

Annie showed Alice the midnight blue sweater and asked, "Do you think he'll like it?"

"Annie, you know Ian will love anything you make for him, even if you were to crochet him a pair of pink and purple socks."

Annie laughed. "Well, I'm not going to do that! I'm saving pink and purple socks to give to you."

"Ha!" Alice said, snickering. "What else have you made for Christmas?"

Annie laid out scarves, mittens, slippers, afghans, caps, and dishcloths on the floral sofa.

"Which is mine?" Alice said, grinning wickedly as she eyed the assortment of winter goods.

"Do you see any pink and purple socks here?" Annie teased. She hoped Alice would love the lavender shell afghan she'd made for her. It was already wrapped in shiny red-and-green foil, with a wide, white ribbon bow. It seemed to Annie that wrapping and unwrapping gifts was a large part of the fun of Christmas and birthdays. Gift bags were lovely, but they certainly kept the fun and suspense of opening presents to a minimum. She rarely used them.

"I'm nearly finished with the crocodile-stitch shawl I'm making LeeAnn," she said. "I hope to mail their gifts early next week. I should have mailed them earlier, I guess, but I just couldn't seem to stop making things for them. Every time I got John's gift finished, I'd think of something else for Joanna. And it just went on and on." She let her voice trail for a bit as she thought of how much she missed the kids, and then how much she missed LeeAnn being little. It especially came home to her how much she missed being an all-the-time mother and grandmother instead of a halfway-across-the-country one. It would have been nice to spend the holidays with her family, but it wouldn't happen this year.

Fearing Alice would sense her change in mood, Annie forced a bright smile and said, "I still need to finish the granny-square afghan for Reverend Wallace and his wife. Last September, I overheard June tell someone that they'd received a granny-square afghan as a wedding gift, and how much they'd both loved it. They lost it when their first house burned down."

"Oh, that's a shame. But I bet they'll love the one you made."

"I hope so."

Alice fingered one of the scarves and then slid a sideways look at Annie.

"You know, if you want to be altruistic, I think maybe Sara Downs could use help more than that old man on the beach."

"Oh?" Annie folded Ian's sweater neatly.

"Did you notice how she was dressed?" Alice asked. "Her shoes were worn out."

"I noticed."

"And her clothes didn't fit," Alice said.

"She looks thin," Annie agreed.

"Yes. And lonely."

"Well, yes," Annie again agree. "She does."

"So … I think if you're going to worry about taking care of someone," Alice concluded, "Sara would appreciate it far more than that old geezer recluse."

"I'd be happy to help Sara if she's willing," Annie said. "Have a seat, and let me get a fire started. How about a refill on your coffee?"

"That would be great," Alice said, "but I'll fill our cups while you tend to the fire. This is a day for toasting ourselves in front of it, isn't it? I brought my quilt square, and I'm determined to finish it before the Hook and Needle Club meeting Tuesday."

A little later they sat comfortably near the fire in the jade-green armchair and a comfy old rocker that had been a favorite of Gram's.

Annie's crochet hook seemed to fly with the yarn as she put the last row on LeeAnn's silvery shawl. Alice chewed on her lower lip as she industriously cross-stitched a representation of the multipaned glass door of the library.

"All I have left after I get this door finished is the little brass plaque beside it," Alice noted.

Annie paused to admire her friend's fine needlework. "It's absolutely beautiful," she said. "I think our quilt will be admired for many years."

"Yes, hanging in the entry hall of the Town Hall, everyone will be able to see it. I'm glad they're going to put it behind glass. Can you imagine how dusty and dirty it would get eventually, what with people coming and going out the front door all the time?"

They worked in silence for a time.

"Do you know where Sara lives?" Annie asked.

"As I said before, I know nothing about her, except that she works at the diner."

"At least she has a job. That's a good thing."

"Maybe she's just getting settled in," Alice said, after a minute or two.

"Very likely."

Another minute passed.

"If it wasn't such a rotten day, we could invite her here for supper."

They both looked out the window at the sleet and snow that came down in such abundance. In unison, they sighed heavily.

"No one is going anywhere for a while," Annie said. "In fact, you may as well plan on spending a couple of days here."

Alice grinned real big. "I was hoping you'd suggest that. I brought my PJs and toothbrush."

"So where are they? In your coat pocket?"

Alice laughed, got up and went to the front door. She returned a moment later with an overnight case and a large tote bag.

Annie stared at the bags and her friend's half-embarrassed expression, and then she burst out laughing.

"What—you didn't want to be alone—snowed in—in the carriage house, I take it."

"You take it right. I just don't trust my furnace, and I think the wiring is going a little dodgy now. Last night, right in the middle of *I Was a Male War Bride* on TCM, everything in the living room and my bedroom went off. I was tired, so I decided to turn in, but then everything came back on at four this morning. I don't appreciate being awakened at 4 a.m. by a blaring television." She put her overnight case aside, sat down, and picked up her quilt square. "This will be nice, Annie. I brought a loaf of bread I made last night and a keg of vegetable stew for lunch."

"Great! I bought some of that good cheddar at the market. We'll have grilled cheese sandwiches and stew for lunch."

The rest of that day and Sunday, Annie and Alice stayed busy and happy, snowed in at Grey Gables.

About mid-afternoon on Sunday Mary Beth Brock called.

"Hi, Annie. Do you still have electricity at Grey Gables?"

"Our power is still on," Annie said. At that moment, the CD player filled the front room with soft jazz, and the lamps added their golden yellow glow to the room. "Did you lose yours?"

"Most of Stony Point did. I tried calling Alice, but she doesn't answer her phone, and I'm worried."

"Oh, she's here, safe and sound! We had a sleepover last night, complete with snacks and movies and lots of giggling. We've done a lot of crafting too. You should see Alice's quilt square. It's gorgeous."

"What fun! I wish I could've joined you."

"That would have been great, Mary Beth. Why not come now if you can get out? Alice is going to whip up a hot-fudge cake, and I'm going to make snow ice cream."

"Oh, that's sounds delicious!" Mary Beth said. "Thanks for inviting me, but I can't get out of my driveway."

"That's too bad. It would be fun, the three of us."

Mary Beth laughed. "Sometimes it seems we girls never outgrow a party, do we?" She laughed again and then continued, "The other reason I called you: Have you heard the latest about our Stony Point Secret Santa Claus?"

"Alice told me earlier about Bud Favor's motorcycle. Isn't that great?"

"Yes, it is. But that's not the latest."

"You mean someone else has received a gift?"

Alice lifted her head sharply, looking at Annie with open expectation.

"Yes! Reverend Wallace went to check on the church

building this morning—we didn't have services because the roads are icy, but you know our pastor. He wanted to be there just in case anyone showed up. Well, at some point between yesterday morning and this morning before he arrived …" she paused dramatically, "someone dropped a large manila envelope of money through the brass mail slot in the front door."

"What?" Annie sputtered in surprise. "Oh, my goodness! How wonderful!"

Alice's eyes brightened with growing curiosity, and she squirmed forward in her chair. "What?" she mouthed. Annie held up one hand, stalling her questions.

"How much money was in it?" Annie asked. Alice put down her cross-stitch and got up.

"Would you believe it matched the exact amount we need to replace the roof?"

Annie took this in. That meant several thousand dollars because the old shingles needed to be removed, and J.L. Roofing—the company that had inspected the roof a few weeks previously—said it appeared some of the decking would have to be replaced as well.

"I think that's the best news I've heard in a long time!" she said.

Alice now stood beside her, fidgeting and mouthing "What? What?" like an eager eight-year-old. Annie grinned at her.

"It's great," Mary Beth agreed. "And it makes you wonder what other blessings are coming, doesn't it?"

"It really does," Annie said. "News like this warms my heart. Keep me informed, Mary Beth, will you?"

"I will, Annie. And now, I better go stir my chowder before it scorches. You and Alice have fun—and stay warm!"

"You too. Thanks for calling!"

She hung up, and Alice grabbed her hand.

"OK! Spill it! Did the mysterious Santa leave another gift?"

"Indeed he did—enough money at the church for the roof to be replaced. Reverend Wallace found it this morning. Apparently someone slipped it through the old mail slot in the front door sometime between yesterday morning and the time he found it today."

Alice clapped her hands in excitement. "That's so great! Oh, I know how much the church has needed a new roof. God bless our secret giver!"

They returned to their chairs and their handiwork, chattering about the church, the old-fashioned door with its built-in slot for mail, and the leaks in various places that discolored the ceiling.

Suddenly Annie's hands stilled and the yarn lay forgotten for a moment between her fingers.

"Alice," she said, "who would have known the exact amount of money that was needed to fix that roof?"

"Reverend Wallace and the church board," Alice said as she continued to industriously push her needle and floss through the image of a cardinal in a snowy pine tree. She paused, looking up at her friend. "Also the roofing company, and probably anyone from the church who asked. Why?"

Annie's eyes were narrowed in thought.

"Because that gift was the *exact* amount needed, so that means ...."

Alice stopped her own handwork.

"That means our mysterious Santa is someone familiar with the details of the church!"

"Right."

"But, Annie," Alice leaned forward slightly, "who in the church has that kind of money? Reverend Wallace?"

"Oh, I hardly think so. Besides, he's the one who found the money."

"Well, he might have *said* he found the money so no one would suspect him."

Annie shook her head. "Reverend Wallace wouldn't lie. And besides, if he had funds like that, the church wouldn't have gone so long with a leaky roof."

"That's true," Alice said with a sigh. She named members of the church board. "None of them have the kind of money that's been spent around here lately," Alice concluded.

Annie sighed with her and picked up her crochet hook.

"At least no one can say it was me this time. I was here with you this whole time."

"No, you weren't!" Alice retorted. "When I showed up yesterday, you had been out already. You might have gone down to the church yesterday morning before I got here. You were still dressed in going-out clothes."

Annie stared at her friend.

"I cannot believe you entertained the thought—even for a half-second—that I gave away a vast amount of money that I don't have."

Alice smiled a smile that seemed to carry a bit of a secret and a lot of a smirk.

"So you say. But no one knows for sure—now do we?"

Annie continued to stare at her in disbelief. "That's crazy talk, and I don't want to hear any more of it."

Alice laughed, made a little locking gesture in front of her lips, giggled again, and then she returned to her cross-stitching.

Alice's reaction further cemented in Annie's mind the need to uncover the identity of the real Stony Point Secret Santa. It simply was not right to be credited for something so generous and lovely when she had nothing whatsoever to do with any of it. One thing about it, though, she'd have to investigate it on her own. Apparently Alice would be no help.

~5~

*M*onday morning when Annie got up and opened her curtains, the sun glared off brilliant glistening snow, and the sky above was so blue it looked nearly brittle. It wasn't the blinding sunlight that woke her up that morning, though. It was the sound of a snow plow in her driveway.

"What on earth?" Alice said, disheveled and yawning as she stood in Annie's bedroom doorway. She shambled across the floor in her fuzzy slippers and yawned again.

"Someone is clearing my driveway," Annie said in amazement. "Who is that?"

"Wow, it's bright out there!" Alice squinted at the machine and its driver. "I can't tell. Don't you know?"

Annie shook her head. "I didn't ask anyone to do that."

"Hmm. Odd." Alice yawned again and scruffed her hair. "Wish he'd clear mine."

"Well, this is one mystery I can solve ASAP," Annie declared, turning from the window. "I'm going out there and asking him!"

"In your pajamas?" Alice said, sounding appalled.

"In my pajamas and coat and boots and gloves. If I get dressed, he'll be finished and gone before I get out there. He's almost finished now!"

She rushed into her wraps and boots and hurried

outside, catching the driver just as he made his final run down the driveway.

He saw her, stopped, and waited.

"Hello!" she shouted over the sound of the tractor's engine.

He nodded once.

"Thank you for clearing my driveway, but I didn't order this service."

"I'm just doing what I was told," he said. "My boss said clean Grey Gables's driveway, and that's what I'm doing."

"Who's your boss?"

"Gil Landry, of course," he said in a tone that suggested she should have known.

"I don't know him. Why did he tell you to plow my snow?"

"Ma'am," he said, "I got a lot of other people's driveways to clear and a couple of parking lots. Maybe you ought to call Mr. Landry."

He put the tractor in gear and raised a hand in farewell.

"My goodness," Annie said, shivering as she watched him drive away. "How odd." Then, she ran after him, yelling, "Wait! Wait!"

He stopped just as he reached the end of her driveway.

"Did your boss tell you to clean the driveway to the carriage house?" she asked.

"Where?"

She pointed. "There. Right next door."

"No, ma'am."

"Would you, please?"

"Clear it?"

"Yes," Annie said.

"Sorry. I wasn't told to."

"Listen," she said, shivering harder. "I'll pay for it. Tell Mr. Landry to send me the bill."

"Well ..." he said. She could see he was going to turn her down.

"I'll include a nice tip for you."

"Well, all right," he said, looking away as if pondering. "And if Mr. Landry gets mad at me, I'm blaming you."

"Now why would he get mad at you for making him more money?"

It was plain to see he had not thought of that. A quick, small smile crossed his face.

"All right. Good day, ma'am."

Annie hurried along her nicely cleared driveway and up the front-porch steps. Alice stood in the door, hands chaffing her crossed arms as if she were the one out in the cold.

"My goodness, Annie, you look half-frozen. Come in and get some hot coffee in you."

"I plan to!" Annie said with as much enthusiasm as her chattering teeth would allow.

In the warm kitchen, Alice poured Annie a huge mug of steaming coffee and set about to making pancakes.

"So? What did he say?" she asked a short time later.

"He said his boss told him to." Alice raised both eyebrows and Annie shrugged. "That's what he said. His boss is Gil Landry. Do you know him?"

"I know who he is," Alice said, "but don't know him personally." She broke eggs into a bowl and beat them with a fork. "Maybe," she said in a sly tone, "he has a crush on you, and this is his way of showing he cares."

"Oh, brother. Don't start that nonsense," Annie said. "Anyway, it's hardly the case, I think, especially as your drive is getting plowed too."

Alice nearly dropped the bowl of eggs.

"What? Mine?"

"Um hmm." Annie sipped her coffee and did not meet her friend's gaze. She wasn't about to reveal her own hand in this situation. Let Alice enjoy her own anonymous gift.

"Well, my goodness." Alice stirred vanilla and sugar into the eggs. "Do you suppose Stony Point's Santa had something to do with it?"

Annie took another drink of her bracing hot coffee, feeling her insides begin to thaw. "I don't know, but I have every intention of finding out."

Later that day—after Annie drove Alice home to save her friend from tromping through two feet of snow that lay on the ground between their two houses—she made a trip to the market. She had depleted her pantry when she gave food to the old man on the beach. The store was busy with shoppers who seemed to have completely run out of staples in the last two days. *Why does that always seem to happen right before and right after a heavy snow?* Annie wondered.

"Hello, Annie," said a cultured voice behind her as she worked her way through the dairy section. "How are you on such a crisp morning?"

She turned and looked into the smiling face of Gwen Palmer.

"Oh hi, Gwen. I'm doing great. Looks like we've had our first major snow of the season, doesn't it?"

"Oh yes," the other woman agreed, reaching for a gallon of skim milk. "And John is still up in Albany. I hope he gets home today." She laughed lightly. "You know, it gets rather lonely in the house when he's not there."

Annie smiled. "I'm sure it does."

"Does it ever bother you?" Gwen asked. "Being home alone all the time, I mean?"

"I still miss Wayne terribly," Annie admitted, wistfully thinking of her late husband. Wayne was taken much too soon over three years earlier. "I guess being alone is just something a person finally grows accustomed to. The funny thing is, the stormy days, or the snowy ones, are the days I miss him the most. We didn't have a lot of winter weather in Texas, so I'm not sure why the Maine winters affect me more than normal."

"Maybe it's the change, reminding you that you're truly in a different place now."

Annie considered it. "You know, you may have a point," she said. "But at least this storm was tolerable. Alice spent the last couple of days and nights at Grey Gables. It was actually fun being snowbound together."

"I'm sure it was," Gwen said. "Alice can be a lot of fun." She glanced around at the shoppers. "I'm surprised so many people were able to get out today."

Annie followed her gaze. "Me too. I wouldn't be here if it hadn't been for someone having my driveway cleared." Gwen raised one perfectly shaped eyebrow. "I woke up this morning, and a snow plow was clearing my driveway for me," Annie explained. "Someone sent a service to do it."

"Really? Why, how wonderful for you. We have a service that does ours, so it's really something I never think much about. I'm so glad you got yours cleared, Annie."

"I was just thinking ... I wonder if whoever did that for me also did it for others."

"It's certainly possible," Gwen said as she picked up a carton of eggs. "Good deeds seem to be the order of the day lately."

"Yes. I heard about Reverend Wallace finding an envelope of money at church yesterday."

Gwen nodded. "Wasn't that marvelous?"

"Yes. It's amazing that someone has been so generous," Annie said. She paused, and then asked, "Gwen, do you happen to know anything about these recent gifts, or who might have been plowing snow for people today?"

"No, I haven't a clue." Gwen looked a little surprised, and she lowered her voice a little. "Have you heard something?"

"Not really. Except that some people suspect that *I've* been doing it—which is ridiculous, of course. But I thought that you might know something."

"I don't know what gave you that idea." A tiny frown flickered across Gwen's smooth brow. "Why would you think that, Annie?"

Annie sensed Gwen raising a barrier. She did not want to pry further and risk offending her friend.

"Only that you're involved in so many activities in the community, much more so than I am, and I thought you may have gotten wind of something."

"Well, I haven't," Gwen said, "and now I need to finish my shopping and get back home. If John returns today, he'll want a nice dinner. See you at the Hook and Needle Club meeting tomorrow."

She hurried away, and Annie couldn't help but feel that she'd blundered across Gwen's invisible barrier. She sighed as she returned to her own shopping list. Gwen did not seem at all surprised when Annie mentioned that others suspected her—Annie Dawson—of being Stony Point's Santa.

— 6 —

When she got home, Annie packed yet another bundle of food. This time she included candles and matches, and a few paperback books. She wrapped up against the cold and once more made the trek to the old man's shack. If she kept him supplied with food, he'd not have to brave the cold to fish for his meals.

Smoke rising from his chimney assured her he was inside, and this time, she left her offering on his stoop without knocking. Given time, perhaps he'd understand she was only concerned for his welfare and had no other intentions than to be a good neighbor. As she walked away, Annie had the strong sensation that he watched her leave the cove.

That night, after she went to bed, Annie lay in the dark and thought about what Alice had said about Sara Downs needing some help. Maybe Alice was right; Sara might need help more than the old man. At the Hook and Needle Club meeting the next day—if Sara was there—Annie would pay closer attention to the woman. If Sara needed help, Annie wanted to help her. But maybe all Sara needed was a job, a place to stay, and some friends. Right now, it seemed as if she was well on her way to having all those. One thing about it, however: Annie would not dismiss the old man from her thoughts and prayers— or her deeds.

*   *   *   *

The next day, Annie was one of the first women to arrive at A Stitch in Time.

"Good morning, Annie," Kate called, almost before Annie had stepped into the place. "Isn't the snow lovely? All my life, I've seen lots of snow, but it's still one of my favorite sights. If you get a storm that has sleet mixed in, it creates such beautiful, vivid sparkles. Of course, the ice makes roads and sidewalks treacherous, but with time, you learn how to deal with it."

They both stared out the large front window for a moment. On a day that was as frigid and sunny as the day before, the drifted snow looked like thousands of diamonds strewn atop mounds of white velvet.

"We never had snow like this in Brookfield," Annie said, removing her wraps. "If we got any, it melted quickly. I have to say, as much as I love the weather down South, I think the snow is gorgeous!"

Kate smiled at her. "I'm so glad you're here today, Annie. I'm afraid some of our group won't show up. Stella, for instance. She needs to stay safely inside when we have ice."

"It would be a shame if she slipped and fell," Annie agreed.

"Yes it would—" Kate broke off, staring outside almost in disbelief. "Well, there she is! Let's hope Jason keeps her from falling."

They watched as Jason, her driver, carefully parked Stella's white Lincoln and then got out and opened the door for her. The car was at least ten years old, but it looked as if it had just been driven off the showroom floor.

"I love Stella, and I think Jason is just wonderful," Kate said in a slight undertone, "but I have to admit the music from *Driving Miss Daisy* plays through my mind every time I see them getting in or out of that car."

The two women watched in silence as Jason held out his hand and helped Stella from the backseat. He hung on to her right hand with his own and cupped her elbow with his free hand. If she slipped and fell, he'd either catch her or go down with her.

"She always looks so elegant," Annie said.

"Yes," Kate sighed. "I hope I look half that good when I'm in my eighties."

Just as the pair stepped cautiously onto the sidewalk, the store door opened and Sara Downs entered. She brought with her a strong gust of cold air and the distinct odor of diner cooking.

"Good morning, Sara!" Annie and Kate said warmly, almost in unison.

She gave them a warm, shy smile.

"Hi." She held up a wrinkled plastic sack with the logo of a large discount store. "I brought my crocheting, but I can only stay an hour. If it weren't for Peggy, I wouldn't be able to come at all. But she talked to Jeff yesterday, and he agreed to one hour."

The door opened right behind her, and she moved aside quickly, as if she were accustomed to getting out of the way. Stella stepped in, casting an annoyed glance at Sara, as if she were indeed in Stella's path.

"My stars," Stella grumbled, "why would anyone get out to attend a meeting on a day as cold as this?"

"Umm," Annie said, eyeing the woman. "Why don't you tell us, Stella?" she asked with a smile.

Jason slid a sideways glance at Annie and another at Stella, who stopped in her tracks and studied Annie's face.

"If you weren't smiling, one might think you were serious, Annie Dawson," she said.

Annie laughed. "But I'm smiling, Stella, and merely giving you a gentle ribbing. We were wondering if you'd venture out today."

"I never let a little thing like snow or bad weather keep me home. We do live in Maine, after all."

Sara was sidling away, but Annie stopped her.

"Stella, have you met Sara Downs? She was here last week, but I wasn't sure you had the opportunity to speak with her. Let's all sit down and get acquainted."

She hoped that putting the women together on a level playing field, such as the Hook and Needle Club meetings, would draw out Sara, loosen up Stella, and make the meetings even more pleasant.

The three of them sat down together as Kate went to answer the phone. Kate and Mary Beth rarely got the chance to sit and work with the other ladies for long stretches because the store remained open during meeting time. Walk-in customers and those on the telephone were always attended to—promptly and with great courtesy. A moment later, Peggy breezed in with a cheerful greeting, and right behind her came Alice. Gwen entered before the other two had hung up their coats.

"Annie," Alice said as she settled, "I left the Mustang at the garage for its regular maintenance, but the mechanic said it would be later this afternoon before it would be ready. May I ride home with you, and then ask you to run me to the garage when they call?"

"No problem," Annie said. She turned to Sara. "Alice lives next door to me."

"Oh, that's nice you have a friend so close," the woman said, smiling.

"It is." Annie wondered if Sara had a good friend somewhere, but she said nothing.

"So," Stella said after everyone settled and as she plucked a half-finished blue slipper out of her tote bag, "where do you live, Sara?"

Sara looked at her, smiled tentatively and said, "In the Atlantic Jewel for now. Maybe I can find a nice apartment soon."

Stella stiffened almost imperceptibly. The Atlantic Jewel was a rundown motel on the outskirts of town. It provided inexpensive lodging but little else. There had been talk a year or so ago of tearing it down or refurbishing it, but no one had made a move one way or another.

"Are you ... *comfortable* there?" Stella asked. Annie could tell the older woman was trying to be courteous, even caring.

"Yes, ma'am," Sara said as she began to crocheting with thin, delicate thread. "It's kinda drab and depressing, but it's warm and comfortable. And clean."

"Do you have kids?" Annie asked as she took out her finished quilt block.

"A grown daughter." Sara drew her lips tight and seemed

totally focused on the piece of lace in her hand. Of course, that look of concentration might also be interpreted as evasive or even closed off.

"Where does she live?" Kate asked from her place at a nearby counter.

Sara stitched faster than ever, and Annie knew then that talk of the woman's daughter agitated her. Annie quickly changed the subject. "Sara, what lovely work you do! What's this going to be?"

Sara gave her a look of relief and gratitude. "I thought I'd make bookmarks to sell," she said. "I've got several to choose from." Uncertainty crossed her face. "Do you think anyone would want to buy one?" She rummaged in her plastic sack. "I brought a few with me … just in case."

"I certainly will buy some! I always need bookmarks." Annie said stoutly. She looked over Sara's bent head at Stella. "You will too, won't you, Stella?"

Stella gave her a startled look, as if Annie had shouted at her. Annie was fairly certain she had not shouted. She may have spoken rather forcefully, but she had not been loud.

Stella cleared her throat and sat even straighter. "Of course," she said, her knitting needles clicking rapidly. I'm happy to support others' endeavors."

"I need bookmarks too," Alice said. "I'm always misplacing mine and resorting to a tissue, or a piece of thread, or whatever is handy. Once I used a candy wrapper." She made a face. "That was a mistake."

Sara retrieved a fistful of limp, lacy bookmarks from the sack.

"I'll have to mix a stiffener for them, of course. Maybe I'll attach ribbons to some of them. What do you think, Annie?" she asked eagerly.

Annie put aside her own work and smoothed several of Sara's ecru-thread bookmarks in her lap. They were incredibly beautiful and delicate, with patterns of roses, birds, and butterflies.

"These are absolutely gorgeous!" she said. "Did you create these designs?"

The woman smiled, ducking her head. "Well, once I had made a few of them with a pattern, I just sort of started making up my own."

"Let me see one of those, please!" Kate said, eagerly snatching a couple from Annie's lap.

"Kate's a killer-diller crocheter too," Annie explained to Sara. "She often creates her own patterns."

"Oh, that's nice," Sara said softly, smiling.

Kate examined the lacy bookmarks. At last she looked at Sara with genuine admiration shining in her eyes. "Oh, Sara! You are a gifted artist! I'll surely buy some of these, and I'll talk to Mary Beth about putting some at the sales counter in the shop."

Before the meeting had even begun, every bookmark Sara brought with her had been spoken for.

"I'll block and stiffen them before the meeting next week," she said. "Thank you so much!"

When she left to go back to work, the women were surprised not to see Peggy hustling out the door at the same time. "Nope," Peggy told the ladies, "I asked Jeff for the day off. I'm planning on a little 'me time' this afternoon."

That being said, the topic turned once again to Sara's lovely workmanship.

"Well, I hardly see how she's going to sell those things to anyone but us," Stella said. "Who buys bookmarks these days when you can get them for free at the library?"

Alice laughed at that. "Stella," she said, "you're so funny sometimes! Have you ever actually looked at the bookmarks they give away at the library? Most of them are advertisements for some business or another. I saw a stack on the circulation desk the other day from a funeral home Down East. I mean, really!" She looked around at the others who nodded and laughed with her.

Stella sniffed. "Well, it was just a thought. I hope that poor woman doesn't think she's going to make a living making those little things."

Alice and Annie exchanged a glance, but Kate was the one who spoke up.

"I was on the phone a couple of times, so I didn't hear everything that was said. Did Sara say she planned to make bookmarks for a living?"

Looking at Kate's pretty eyes and her questioning expression, Annie doubted Kate's question was as serious as her voice sounded. But Stella never looked up from her stitching.

"She didn't say that," Gwen said, "but I'm sure she hopes to make some extra money."

No one spoke for a little bit and then Stella said, to no one in particular, "She surely doesn't have much to say, that one."

Annie stirred a little in her chair. "Maybe she feels uncomfortable."

"Uncomfortable?" Stella glanced up long enough to frown over the rims of her glasses. "Why on earth would she feel uncomfortable? We're a personable group of women. We welcomed her into our circle."

Mary Beth cleared her throat.

"Yes, and she's going to be an asset, I believe. Now, we haven't mentioned the quilt yet, but I want you to know that all of you have made me proud with your hard work. Thanks for your participation and for bringing in your finished quilt blocks over the last few days. Peggy gave me hers depicting The Cup & Saucer this morning. That completes all our blocks, so now I'm ready to take it to Barbara Westinghouse as soon as the meeting is over."

The door of the shop opened and a young man in workman's heavy coveralls and a wool cap pulled over his ears entered. He glanced around, looking slightly surprised to see a group of woman sitting in a circle working on needlecrafts. His gaze finally landed on Mary Beth.

"Ms. Brock! Where do you want the refrigerator?"

Every woman in the place held her project immobile and gaped at the young man.

"Refrigerator?" Mary Beth echoed, as if she'd never heard the word before.

"Yes, ma'am. We're parked in the alley by the back door, but it's locked. Tom thought maybe we got our directions mixed up and were to deliver it to your home."

"What?" Mary Beth said weakly. Then she rallied and said, "You're mixed up, I think, Brad. I didn't order a refrigerator for here, or for my house."

He merely looked at her and shrugged. "I'm sorry,

Ms. Brock. I'm just doing what I was told to do, and that was to deliver a refrigerator to you." An expression crossed his face, and he blushed a little as he pulled something from his pocket. He said, "I forgot. I was supposed to give this to you."

He handed her a small envelope. While everyone watched with curiosity and anticipation, Mary Beth broke the seal and took out a square, white card and read the words aloud: "This gift is for you to enjoy. Merry Christmas, from Stony Point's Santa."

Mary Beth plunked down suddenly in the chair nearest her, next to Gwen who gazed at her from wide, happy eyes.

"Mary Beth!" Kate and Peggy said in unison, excitement in their voices.

"I can hardly believe it!" Alice said, and Annie exclaimed, "It's just what you needed!"

Stella shook her head.

"Who on earth is giving these gifts?" she asked.

"Mary Beth, how wonderful!" Gwen said, her fingers on the woman's forearm. "You aren't going to faint, are you?"

"No," Mary Beth said weakly. "No, I don't think so. Oh, my."

"Here," Kate said, handing her a glass of water.

They waited as she drank deeply. "Oh, my," she said again.

"Can you unlock that back door, Ms. Brock?" the delivery boy said, grinning.

Mary Beth looked at him, dazed.

"I'll get it, Brad," Kate said. She patted Mary Beth's head and then hurried to the back door.

"Now," said Peggy, "you won't have to worry any more about food spoiling when you have it here."

A little later, after the men had unloaded and installed the refrigerator in the corner of the storage room, the women tromped into the back to admire it. Small and sleek, its stainless steel sides gleaming in the overhead light, the refrigerator gave an air of elegance to the place where boxes of yarn, craft books, needles, buttons, and other crafting miscellanea were neatly stored.

"It's just the right size for that space," Mary Beth breathed.

"And now you need a nice little dinette to go with it," Alice said, "and maybe a soft little armchair and ottoman so you can put up your feet during breaks."

"I'd give you my little table, because we have really outgrown it, but if I did that, where would we eat?" Peggy said gaily as she ran her palm along the cool steel. "Besides, two of the chairs have been broken. Wally fixed them as best he could, but I wouldn't want to give them away. What if one broke when you sat on it?" She laughed. "We don't want Mary Beth or Kate ending up on the floor!"

Mary Beth laughed and hugged Peggy. "Thank you for the thought," she said, "but really, we're fine with our card table and the folding chair."

"That can't be comfortable," Annie said. "I have a small arm chair and ottoman that would fit perfectly in this little nook," she continued. It sat unused in one of the spare rooms at Grey Gables, and it would be ideal for the women to relax in while they enjoyed their breaks.

"Annie ..." Mary Beth said, and Annie saw she was about to protest.

"It's not doing me a bit of good, and I'd love to see it used," she said. "I wish I'd thought of it earlier."

"And I have a sweet little table with two chairs you may have," Stella offered.

"Well, my goodness!" Mary Beth's eyes filled with tears.

— 7 —

"Not many in here today," Alice said as she and Annie settled into a booth covered with dark green vinyl at The Cup & Saucer The green ivy accents and bright yellow cups and saucers in the diner made a pleasant contrast to winter weather. The friends had decided to have lunch together after the Hook and Needle Club meeting.

"Well, no," Annie said with a smile. "Look outside."

Alice twisted her mouth. "Annie, don't you know we Mainers are used to snow? You've lived up here long enough by now."

Annie sighed. "I know. White Christmas and all, huh?"

"Usually," Alice said as a waitress—not Peggy since she took the day off—brought menus.

They each ordered clam chowder and hot tea—something to warm them from the inside out, as Gram would have said.

Alice gave her friend a sharp look.

"Annie, how did Stony Point's Santa know that Mary Beth's fridge stopped working?"

Annie shrugged. "I have no idea, but isn't it great? What a darling little refrigerator ...." She let her voice trail and narrowed her eyes, staring at Alice. "I hope you're not thinking what I think you're thinking, because if you are, you can think again. I had nothing to do with that!"

Alice raised one eye brow in the most maddening way.

"I just heard you give away a perfectly good chair and ottoman."

"And Stella, who can sometimes be a little tightfisted, gave Mary Beth a table and chairs. It's the season of giving, Alice."

Alice blinked. "She did! Maybe *she's* Stony Point's Santa."

Annie had been thinking the same thing, although Stella seemed about as far from being Santa Claus as anyone she could think of.

"Well, all I can say is I hope none of the other women in the club think I'm the person behind this secret gift-giving," Annie said.

Alice sort of shrugged, and her suspicious little smile once again irked Annie a bit.

"Listen. I'm saying this again: I'm not taking credit for giving away money, motorcycles, refrigerators, or anything else that's being done anonymously. When I give gifts, it's obvious, just like with the chair and ottoman. OK?"

Alice grinned. "OK."

But Annie was fairly certain her friend still wasn't persuaded.

Just before they left, Sara came out of the kitchen, a large white apron wrapped around her tiny frame and her lank hair caught back in a hairnet. She pushed a cart and bussed tables, but she did not see Annie and Alice on the opposite side of the room.

"I like Sara a lot," Annie said as they watched her remove plates from the first table. "There is a true artist and a warm heart in that tired little body."

Alice nodded. "She's awfully shy, but I think she'll warm up to us as time goes on."

"Oh, yes!" Annie said with a smile. "Did you see how enthusiastic she was when she started talking about her bookmarks?"

"Those were *gorgeous*! I loved all the patterns, so I'm going to buy several of them."

"Me too. You know, the twins need bookmarks. And LeeAnn has always been a big reader."

"If Sara took them to Dollie Bracken's Gift Boutique, I bet Miss Dollie would buy them from her," Alice said. "Her shop carries such lovely, elegant items."

"Yes! And so would The Gift Gallery in Portland," Annie added.

"And there's that bookstore in Portland too—Books Galore," said Alice. "These would fit right in there."

The two women grinned at each other like a couple of co-conspirators, all but rubbing their hands in anticipation.

"Shall we tell her now?" Alice asked as they watched Sara move to the next table.

"No, let's not yet," Annie said.

Alice frowned. "Why not?"

"Because if those businesses don't want to sell her bookmarks, then Sara would never need to know. I'd hate to build up her hopes just to crush them." She gazed at Sara as she dipped a dishcloth in a small container of water, wrung it out, and wiped off the table.

"You're right," Alice said in an undertone as their new friend grew nearer.

Sara looked from her work, smiling when she saw Annie and Alice. Raising one hand, she offered a tentative wave before finishing with the table. When she finally reached the two women, she smiled again.

"Hi! I didn't know you two would be in today."

"We often come for a bite of lunch after the Hook and Needle Club meeting," Annie said.

Alice added, "It's one of our favorite things to do!"

Sara nodded and glanced around. "It's a nice place. This is probably the best job I've ever had. The boss is real nice, and the waitresses treat me with respect. I like that."

It was obvious by Sara's downtrodden demeanor that she'd rarely been shown respect. Annie just wanted to hug her with all the pent-up maternal energy she had, even though Sara was probably her age or even a little older. She settled for touching the woman's forearm with her fingertips and smiling at her warmly.

"I'm so glad you like your job," Annie said. "I do believe this is a great place to work. It's certainly a fine place to eat."

Sara smiled, nodded, and started to move on, but Annie stalled her again.

"Could you do something for me?" she asked.

"I'll try."

"I know you have your bookmarks with you because you came straight here from the meeting—right?"

Sara nodded.

"Would you be willing to let me borrow two or three of them, just to look at for a while? Maybe, at some point, you can teach me some of those patterns, and I can use them in an afghan."

"Oh, sure!" Sara said. "I'd be happy to."

She left and returned a minute later with three bookmarks.

"Here they are. Keep them as long as you need to, Annie." She met Annie's eyes and smiled with genuine friendship.

"Thanks!" Annie looked at the bookmarks; one contained an image of a hummingbird, another had roses, and the remaining one had praying hands. She was sure these would be ideal for her true purpose in asking to borrow them. "You know, Sara, you'll have to come over to Grey Gables sometime, and we'll have a little crochet party."

"Hey!" Alice said. "What about me?"

Annie looked at her friend and laughed. "You can bring your cross-stitch. Maybe we'll have another pajama party."

"On New Year's Eve. Let's do it!" Alice said. "What do you think, Sara?"

Sara ducked her head. "That would be fun," she murmured. "Peggy says Grey Gables is really beautiful."

"Then I'll take you on the grand tour when you visit," Annie said, her arms spread out dramatically.

"That would be nice," Sara said again. "Well, I have to get back to work now. You ladies have a nice day."

As soon as they were out of The Cup & Saucer, Alice said, "You are a wily woman, Annie Dawson, the way you got those bookmarks."

"Well, not altogether wily," Annie said. "I *do* want to examine the patterns and see if I can't translate them into a piece made with yarn. But the main purpose is so I'll have something to show Miss Dollie. Shall we go there now?"

"Let's do. But it's not that far, and the sidewalk is almost clear. Let's walk."

"All right! I need the exercise."

"Me too!" Alice agreed.

Annie wondered if there was ever a woman their age who did not say, frequently, "I need the exercise." When they reached the boutique, Annie read aloud the sign posted on the door, "Closed until April 1st."

"Oh no!" she said in disappointment. "I'm sure Miss Dollie would have ordered some bookmarks."

"I suppose business is bad if she's closed during the holidays. But maybe things will pick up in the spring when the tourists return."

"Let's hope so," Annie said.

Alice agreed, and then said, "We may as well go home. Unless you need to go somewhere else."

"Nowhere here in town, but I do need to take care of something when I get home."

"Oh?"

Annie grinned. "Put your curiosity meter away. It's just a private little matter I need to tend to."

"Uh huh. It's that old man, isn't it? You're going to go chasing after him, aren't you?"

Annie kept walking and did not reply.

"See? See?" Alice taunted her. "By your very silence you're saying yes."

"So what if I am?" Annie said. "I'm just going to make sure he's all right, that's all."

They walked without speaking until they got in Annie's classic Chevy Malibu.

"I just hope he's not some kind of serial killer," Alice said as she fastened her seat belt.

Annie backed out of the parking place.

"I hope he isn't, either."

She said no more on the subject and neither did Alice until Annie stopped to let her friend out at the carriage house.

"How about if I come with you?"

"To check on the old man?"

"Yes."

"No," Annie said.

Alice huffed. "Why not?"

"Because he doesn't want *me* there. I'm sure he doesn't want someone tagging along."

"But what if he pulls a gun or a knife or a machete or something?"

Annie laughed. "He won't. He's old and he's frail."

"Old and frail does not mean he can't squeeze a trigger."

"I'm not worried, Alice. I'm going to go check on him quickly, and as soon as I'm back I'll give you a call, all right?"

Alice narrowed her eyes as if she were a stern parent. "Take your cellphone with you, and I mean it."

Annie laughed, reached over, and surprised her worried friend with a hug. "All right. I will."

"I have a can of mace. You want that?"

"Oh, *Alice!*"

"I'm serious. I can run in and get it for you in a jiffy."

"No. I'm not going to mace some poor old man whom I'm trying to make sure is warm and fed."

"All right." Alice unfastened her seat belt, gathered her

cross-stitch and purse, then got out of the car. "Call me. I mean it."

"I shall. I mean it."

A few minutes later, as Annie faced the cold walk toward the shack, Alice's concerns and warnings clanged in her mind like unwanted noise. If she were totally honest with herself, Annie would have to admit she was a little apprehensive about the old man's ability to harm her. On the other hand, she couldn't look at herself in the mirror if she chose not to follow through on seeing him through the winter—at least as long as he stayed on the beach.

Apparently he had seen her approaching his shack. He opened the door far enough that she could see him.

"I'm fine. Go home. Don't come back."

He shut his door; she heard the lock click. He had looked fine; he had sounded strong. Smoke came from his chimney.

Go home, Annie, she told herself. She turned and retraced her steps to Grey Gables.

— 8 —

The following Monday afternoon, Annie finished the last of the last-minute gifts she'd made for LeeAnn, Herb, and the twins. She wrapped every gift separately and packed them in the two cartons she planned to take to the post office the next day.

After such a busy week, she decided to celebrate by watching *It's a Wonderful Life* on television. She so enjoyed the holidays because of all the heartwarming, fun Christmas movies and programs available. If she wasn't careful, Annie could sit for hours crocheting as she watched holiday movies on the Hallmark Movie Channel or some other family-friendly network.

She put a bag of popcorn in the microwave; then she became aware of an odd sound in another room. She chased down the noise and found that Boots—that dear, sweet cat who was often so warm and lovable—had dug her way through the shredded newspaper in one of the cartons and had clawed away half the paper on one of Herb's gifts. As Annie watched, Boots tugged on the ribbon of LeeAnn's present as if her survival depended on shredding it.

"*Boots!*"

The cat leaped as though startled, bowed her back, jumped from the box, and skittered sideways as Annie approached.

"Bad kitty!" she said. She kept her voice firm, but low. A scared cat would only make a bigger mess. "Oh, my goodness! Look at what you've done!"

Boots dove beneath the sofa, as if she knew the depth of her transgression and thought "Out of sight, out of mind" might work with her human. With a huff and a glower, Annie got on her knees and gathered sparkling bits of ribbon and shreds of shiny paper.

"Honestly, Boots," she muttered as she plucked up every scrap she could, "what in the world got into you? You're usually such a good cat."

Boots, of course, had nothing to say. In fact, she gazed at Annie with a look of pure annoyance.

Just as Annie reached beneath a table to get what she hoped was the last bit, she smelled something foul. Not only was it foul, it was burning. She recognized it immediately.

"Oh, the popcorn!" she shouted and rushed toward the kitchen. When she and Wayne had used their old-fashioned popcorn popper, or when she was a girl making popcorn in Gram's black iron skillet, it never created such an awful odor when she burned or scorched it. What was the difference between the old-fashioned stuff and the microwave popcorn?

A slightly gray fog hung in the air of the kitchen. Annie opened the door of the microwave. Smoke and stench puffed out at her like dandelion fluff, but luckily, there were no flames. Her eyes stung, and she nearly gagged. She took a dishcloth from the drying rack and gingerly extracted the charred bag. She carried it out the back door and deposited it on the frozen ground where the cold temperature would neutralize the stench.

Back inside, she opened the kitchen window. Frigid fresh air blasted inside as if it had long lingered, pressing against the glass, waiting for an opportunity to invade Grey Gables. Annie grimaced slightly, but she'd rather have the icy breeze than rank odor.

She grabbed a can of air freshener and sprayed every room in the house. As she rewrapped the gifts and then sealed the box for mailing, she hoped she wasn't sending the odor of burned popcorn all the way to Texas. Finally, after closing the window, she took a long warm shower where she scrubbed her hair and scoured her skin until it was bright red.

The next morning, on the way to the Hook and Needle Club meeting, Annie felt as though the smell of burnt popcorn still permeated her every pore even though she had taken another shower and shampooed her hair again when she'd gotten up.

"My goodness," Mary Beth said when Annie moved her chair slightly away from the group, "do you think we have a germ, or do you have one?"

Stella's head shot up. "Anyone who is ill should not come to the meetings."

Annie laughed as she settled down, pulled a fresh skein of yarn from her tote bag, and began a foundation chain for a new afghan pattern.

"I'm not sick," she said. "In fact, I feel just fine. But I'm afraid I don't smell very good."

"Oh, good grief!" Kate said, giggling and sniffing. "Why? Haven't you had a shower for a while?"

"I've had two! But I burned popcorn last night, and the stench filled the entire house."

Peggy, who sat next to Annie, leaned over and sniffed delicately.

"Hmm. When I burn popcorn it never smells like lavender and tea rose."

Annie lifted her forearm and sniffed the sleeve. "You don't smell that?"

"I don't smell a thing!" Peggy declared.

"Neither do I," said Sara who sat on the other side of Annie.

The rest of women echoed Peggy and Sara's assessments.

Annie smiled at them all gratefully, but she had a feeling they were being kind.

"I left all my windows open just an inch or two because Grey Gables absolutely *reeks*. I know it'll be cold inside, but at least it will smell fresh. I'm going into Portland as soon as the meeting is over."

Stella gave her a sharp look.

"Do you think that's safe, Annie, to leave your windows open that way?"

"I think so. This *is* Stony Point, after all."

"Hmm," Stella said. Then she let out a deep breath and turned back to her work. "I'd certainly never leave my house open for all and sundry."

Annie did not like the direction of this conversation and quickly changed the subject before anyone else could jump in with dire warnings and statistics.

"So, Mary Beth and Kate, how are the two of you liking the little table and chair, and the armchair and ottoman?"

"Oh, Annie, our break area is now so cozy and comfy," Kate said.

"We've hung a few little ornaments on the wall and put down a cute little rug," Mary Beth added. "You all will have to take a look back there before you leave. Again, thank you, Annie and Stella, for your generosity."

"You're so welcome," Annie said.

"Of course you're welcome," Stella added. "I wasn't using that table and chairs, and I'm glad to see them being put to good use."

"So what's the latest report about Stony Point's Santa?" Annie said. "Any more gifts or money given out recently?"

"Mike Malone got a new computer delivered for the purpose of creating a better-quality news sheet," Gwen announced as casually as she might have said, "Mike got a fresh haircut." She continued working on an embroidered Christmas scene.

"My goodness!" Peggy nearly shouted. "When was that?"

"I believe it was late yesterday afternoon, shortly before he closed the hardware store."

"That's wonderful!" Alice said. "I so enjoy reading *The Point*. I'm sure that now it will be even better."

"Yes," Kate said, nodding enthusiastically. "I bet with the new computer, he can archive everything."

"As I understand it," Gwen said, "—and believe me when I say I don't fully understand computers—" She paused while everyone laughed and then continued. "This new computer has some kind of publishing software that has all the bells and whistles the big newspapers use."

"I think that's perfectly lovely!" Annie sighed. "Mike is such a great guy, and he's such an asset to our community. I'm so happy for him."

"Since none of the rest of us had heard about Mike's windfall yet, how'd you hear so soon?" Kate asked Gwen.

"Ouch!" Gwen gasped, putting the tip of her finger in her mouth. "Oh, my!" she said a moment later, looking at it. "Mary Beth, I'm afraid I need a Band-Aid so I don't get any blood on this piece."

While Mary Beth bustled off to fetch the first-aid box, Gwen held her fingertip to her mouth and looked at the others.

"To answer your question, Kate," she said, "Mike called us last night, so excited he could hardly speak. Why, John was as excited as Mike, and he went over to the hardware store so he could admire the new machine." She laughed. "You know, I would have gone, too, but one computer looks pretty much like another to me. And John didn't get home until nearly midnight!"

Mary Beth returned with the first-aid box and opened it as she reached Gwen.

"Here," she said, "let me have your finger." As she tended to Gwen's wound, she said, "I suspect it will take a while for Mike to learn all those bells and whistles you mentioned."

"I'm sure you're right," Gwen agreed. "I think John said something about Mike attending a class in Portland."

"Courtesy of Stony Point's Santa?" Annie asked.

Gwen met Annie's eyes. "No," she said slowly. "I believe John is going to fund it." She glanced at everyone else. "Have you noticed how we all seem to be helping each other more since this mysterious Santa showed up? Not that I'm bragging on John, or saying our town has been miserly, but it's as if some extra spirit of generosity has been poured on Stony Point, and it's spreading."

"Yes!" Alice said. "Like ripples in a pool."

"Oh, I've always liked that analogy!" Kate said, smiling, fluttering her fingers in a gesture of water flowing.

Through most of the conversation, Sara Downs, who sat on Annie's right, had kept her eyes and focus on the work in her hands. Annie paused to watch the little steel crochet hook flash in the light, creating tiny stitches that turned into vines and leaves in a bookmark. The woman worked with intensity, her face drawn tight, her hands as tense as talons. She wore a faded brown shirt with frayed cuffs and old jeans that were too big and cinched at the waist. Her scuffed sneakers had thin, worn soles and mended shoelaces. The ripples of generosity had not reached Sara who undoubtedly needed it as much or more than anyone in the town.

"How are you doing, Sara?" Annie asked.

"Fine," the woman replied, with a quick glance up and brief smile.

Annie caught only a glimpse of the woman's eyes, but she thought she saw worry, or maybe it was fear. Some thought lurked behind the facade, and it made her uneasy.

"Is everything all right?" Annie asked in an undertone as the women around her chatted with one another.

Another swift glance up and back down.

"Yes, fine, thank you, ma'am." She closed her lips tight, perhaps from tension. Or was it a subtle way of telling Annie she had no interest in sharing whatever bothered her? And why should she? Annie and all the women of the club were practically strangers to Sara.

"Oh!" Annie said. "I nearly forgot! I still have those three bookmarks you lent me last week. I want to pay you for them."

"But I haven't washed or blocked them yet, and I need to add the stiffener."

"I'll bring them next week for you to do that, if that's OK with you," said Annie.

Sara nodded. "That'll be fine."

"But it's all right if I pay you now, isn't it?"

Sara smiled and relief leaped into her eyes.

"That would be just fine, thank you."

"I also brought something that I thought you might like," Annie said as she paid the woman for the three bookmarks. She removed a yellow-orange-brown–plaid tote from her project bag.

"I hope you'll take this," she said, shaking it out to reveal its full size and features. "I bought it a few years ago in Texas at a craft fair, and it's just not me. I happened to see it in my closet the other day, and that soft, sweet yellow made me think of your lovely, quiet demeanor."

"Oh!" Sara said, her eyes going large and round as she looked at the beautiful tote bag. She touched it with tentative fingertips. "It's beautiful!" She raised her eyes to Annie. "But you don't want to get rid of it, do you? I mean, it's so fine and all."

"Of course I want to give it to you. Honestly, Sara, I have a dozen tote bags at the house, not counting all the craft baskets and bags Gram had kept over the years. And you know what else? I have about five balls of white crochet thread, size 30. Would you like it? I'm afraid I'm not going to have time to use it until this time next year! I have several yarn projects planned."

"But you'll need the thread later, won't you?"

"Perhaps. But I hate to see the thread get old. You know how fibers can sometimes become fragile after a while. If that happens then I'll just have to throw it all away, and that would be a shame."

"Oh, no! Don't throw it away. I'll take it and make good use of it, I promise."

"I'll bring it by The Cup & Saucer soon," Annie promised.

A look of panic flashed across Sara's face.

"What time is it?" she asked, looking around in what Annie could only describe as alarm. "Oh, what time is it? Am I late?"

"It's almost noon," Kate said.

Sara stuffed her work into her tattered plastic shopping bag and then placed that inside the plaid tote that Annie had given her.

"Oh, I'm going to be late!" she cried, dropping her crochet hook on the floor.

"Here," Peggy said, handing it to her. "You won't get fired for being a couple of minutes late; I promise. Jeff is a good boss."

"I hope you're right because I can't lose my job," she said, clutching everything to her chest. "I just can't!" Without another word she fled from the shop.

Dead silence fell on the club members.

"My goodness," Stella said at last, "I do believe that is the strangest woman I've ever met."

Mary Beth nodded. "I wonder where she's from, and what her story is."

"I don't like that she keeps so much to herself," Gwen said. "I don't mean to sound harsh, but that silent, sneaky look arouses my suspicions."

"The very fact she refuses to talk about herself makes me uncomfortable," Alice added.

"She's very shy," Annie reminded them.

"I don't trust her," Stella said, "and if I sound harsh, then so be it. I'm not so sure we should have welcomed her into this group so quickly, if at all. In fact, if she doesn't become more forthcoming about herself, I recommend we ask her to stay away."

"What?" Annie said. "Really? You never have anything good to say about the woman, Stella, but that remark is truly outrageous!"

Stella huffed in obvious annoyance.

"I'm not surprised you're outraged, Annie, since you're trusting enough to leave home with your windows open."

"Actually, Annie, to be completely fair about what Stella said," Gwen put in, "Sara really is not our kind of people."

Annie felt her eyes grow large, and the ringing in her ears increased.

"Oh my goodness," she squeaked out. Then louder, "Oh my goodness!" She swallowed hard before saying through the sand in her throat, "If you will excuse me, I really must get out of here before I say something I'll regret. But I heartily recommend those of you who look down on Sara to examine your hearts and minds to see if you can find a scrap of the true spirit of Christmas."

Blindly she gathered her crochet, her coat, scarf, and hat, and then she left A Stitch in Time. The stench of their attitudes smelled far worse than the popcorn she had burned the night before. Right then Annie Dawson was not sure she ever wanted to return to the Hook and Needle Club.

~ 9 ~

By the time Annie pulled into her driveway after her trip to Portland, evening had fully fallen, and the stars seemed to pop like sprouts out of the frozen sky. She stood a moment to absorb the rhythm of the ocean waves and the quiet peace of the night.

The conflict earlier in the day at the Hook and Needle Club meeting still rankled Annie when she thought about it. Somehow she must persuade Stella and Gwen to look past Sara's poverty and skittish behavior and into the soul of the woman. Otherwise, she must reconcile herself to the fact that her friends were elitists who would never accept Sara into their midst. If they made that choice, then Annie would have to rethink her own place in that group of women. She wasn't so surprised by Stella's words, but Gwen's surprised her. Even though Gwen had a social position to maintain, Annie thought that Gwen had learned not to judge people unfairly after a similar attitude toward her youngest son's fiancée had almost cost her his trust and affection.

Annie's successful venture into the city on behalf of Sara and her craft had soothed Annie's troubled mind somewhat. She was eager to seek out Sara on Wednesday with the good news of two rather large bookmark orders.

Weary and shivering, leaving her tote bag with her crochet project in it, Annie took groceries from the backseat and then trudged to the house as the wind shoved against her. The steps up to the front porch seemed steeper than usual that night. She paused on the top one and glanced toward the windows. Wind stirred the curtains. She was glad she'd left a light on in the front room, but she wished she'd had the presence of mind to turn on the porch light before she left. She put the groceries on the floor next to the door and fished the key out of her pocket.

It seemed rather foolish to Annie now that she'd bothered to lock the door when she'd left the windows open. She inserted the key and turned it. The door opened silently.

That's what oiling the hinges and having a good handyman like Wally Carson will do for you, she thought with a smile. She was glad she'd asked Wally to come out to Grey Gables a few weeks earlier to check on things like door hinges and weather stripping, the furnace, the oven, and water pipes.

She hoisted the shopping bags into her arms and stepped gratefully over her threshold. She paused long enough to sniff like a bloodhound for the scent of burned popcorn. Even with the windows just barely open, the house was very cold. The air inside the cold house smelled as clean as fresh snow. She closed the door with her foot. With her breath pluming in the chill, Annie walked toward the kitchen when she noticed light spilling into the hallway.

Had she left the light on in there as well as in the front room? She didn't remember doing so, but it was possible, especially given her flurry of activity that morning as she organized her day. The bags were heavy in her arms, and she hurried on, eager to deposit them on the counter. The telephone rang the moment she released the bags.

"Hello?"

"Annie!" It was Alice. "I've been watching for you to get home."

"Hi, Alice," she said, still miffed with her friends, including this one who had not come to Sara's defense. "I just walked in."

"I saw your car lights so I gave you a minute to get in the house. Listen, I want to talk to you. Is it all right if I come over?"

Annie was tired and right then all she wanted was to close the windows, turn up the furnace, have a warm drink, take a hot bath, and crawl into bed.

Annie's response was slow enough that it prodded Alice to speak again. "Please?" she asked. "I ... I'm sorry about what happened at the meeting. All of us talked about it after you left, and we're all so sorry about what happened. In fact, Gwen and Stella both admitted they were out of line. You will forgive us, won't you, Annie?"

Annie sighed. She was tired and annoyed, but she was also loving and forgiving. If Alice wanted to smooth over the churned waters of the Hook and Needle Club, then Annie refused to turn her down.

"Of course," Annie acquiesced. "I'll get some coffee started and turn up the furnace. With the windows being opened all day, it's cold in here."

"I don't mind. I'll be right there."

Annie closed the kitchen window and then quickly put away her groceries. She turned up the thermostat and went from room to room closing windows. In the library, she turned on a small desk lamp. Tucked between the living room and family room, the library seemed warmer than the rest of the house, and when Annie reached to close the first window, she realized why. Apparently, she had neglected to open the library windows that morning. She took in a deep breath, testing for the bad odor. What she smelled was something different.

Peanut butter. *Peanut butter?* In the library?

Annie frowned, sniffing again energetically. She glanced around the dimly lit room, trying to figure out where the scent came from. And when did she leave a pile of laundry in the armchair?

Maybe the cat, in vengeful retaliation for the previous evening's harsh scolding, had somehow gotten in the hamper and dragged out dirty clothes. Even as she concocted an image of Boots toting clothes through the house in her mouth, Annie realized how ridiculous the notion was.

"Boots?" she said, squinting in the dim light at the chair as she moved toward it.

This time the clothing moved, almost as if stirred. Annie's heart leaped, and she froze. She started to reach out for the clothes when she saw a pair of eyes blinking sleepily in a thin, pale face.

"Oh!" she gasped, jumping back in spite of herself.

The knock at the front door made her jump again. She hoped it was her friend.

"Alice?" she called, her voice somewhat tentative.

"Yes!"

"Come in. Hurry!"

Alice opened the door, and the frigid air that entered with her added to the coldness inside Grey Gables.

"Where are you?"

"In the library."

"Is the coffee on? My goodness, it's cold in here! You know, I don't smell any burned—"

She broke off and halted abruptly as she entered the library.

"What ... what's wrong, Annie?"

Annie moved her hand just enough to indicate the bundle in the chair. She dared not take her gaze off whomever it was that looked back at her.

"Oh, my goodness! What's in those blankets?" Alice took a few steps back, gawking, with one hand at her throat.

Annie swallowed hard. "I believe it's a child."

～ 10 ～

"A child!"

Annie still did not take her eyes away from the small person in the chair.

"Turn on the other lamps, would you please, Alice?"

As the warm, golden light filled the room, Annie finally saw what sat in front of her: Wrapped in a worn, pastel pink blanket was a thin little girl with wispy, tangled white-blond hair, a pale face, and huge blue eyes the color of a faded summer sky. With the tiny fingers of one hand, she clutched a tattered teddy bear. She solemnly sucked the thumb of her free hand.

A jar of peanut butter and a spoon lay next to her in the chair.

"My goodness," Annie murmured, staring at the girl.

"Who is she?" Alice asked.

"I don't know. I don't recognize her at all."

"How old do you think she is, Annie?"

"No more than two and a half or three, I'd say. She may be older, but just tiny and frail."

The girl shrank back as Annie approached. Dark smudges beneath the large blue eyes almost looked like bruises.

Annie knelt and rested her hands on the arm of the chair. She smiled gently, looking into those eyes.

"Hi, sweetheart. Can you tell me your name?"

The girl simply stared at her. Annie glanced up at Alice who now stood on the other side of the chair. Alice lifted her shoulders and bit her lower lip. She bent down.

"Where'd you come from, honey?" she asked.

The child blinked, slid her gaze from Annie to Alice, but still she said nothing.

"How in the world did she get in here?" Annie said. "I only left the windows open a crack, and she's far too small to have raised one the rest of the way by herself."

Alice glanced toward the library window.

"Even if she had done that, she'd have to remove a screen. Annie, did you lock your doors this morning when you left?"

"Yes. In fact, as I was unlocking the front door a little bit ago, I was thinking how silly it was to lock the doors when the windows were open."

"Then she had to come in through a window."

"Yes. She didn't magically appear inside Grey Gables."

The little girl shifted in the chair, snuggling down more into the dingy blanket.

"Alice," Annie said, looking at the child, "would you finish closing all the windows for me so the house can get warm? I was shutting them when I saw the light coming from in here."

"Of course." Alice straightened, started to move away and then stopped. "I wonder how long she's been in here."

"I don't know. Long enough to eat this, with this." Annie picked up the small jar of peanut butter and spoon.

"She's probably hungry."

At Alice's words, the little girl turned her head and

looked at Alice with expectation. It was the first sign of any emotion.

"Are you hungry, sweetheart?" Annie asked.

The girl looked at her and nodded.

"For goodness' sake. Well, then, let's get you fed."

Annie reached for her, somewhat tentatively, expecting the girl to shrink back. Instead, the child removed the thumb from her mouth and held out her arms.

Annie smiled and gathered her into her arms.

"Maybe she'll talk after her tummy is full," Alice said.

"Yes. I hope so!"

In the kitchen, Annie settled the little girl in a kitchen chair, snugly tucking the pink blanket around her. She wanted to fix something quick, warm, and nutritious. Perhaps some of the leftover potato soup and a grilled cheese sandwich would fit the bill.

She could hear Alice shutting the windows upstairs. When Alice joined them, Annie was spooning soup into a bowl.

"Alice, would you please get one of the twins' booster seats from the closet under the stairs while I finish fixing her dinner?"

"Sure!" Alice gave the girl a smile and said, "Mmm! Do I smell grilled cheese sandwiches?" The girl blinked at her, but did not speak.

A few minutes later, as the kitchen warmed, Annie settled the little girl into the booster seat, tied a clean dish towel around her neck, and put a bowl of soup, the sandwich, and a glass of milk in front of her. The girl grabbed the milk and gulped it.

"My word!" Annie gasped. "She's been starving for milk!"

"Starving for just about everything from the looks of it," Alice said, filling the glass again.

The two women watched as the child devoured her food.

"Oh, goodness. And look at her eyes. Do you think someone has hit her?"

Annie shook her head. "No. I think she's just frightened, hungry, and very tired. LeeAnn used to get circles around her eyes like that when she was worn out. Plus, when I washed her face and hands I didn't see any bruises or other signs of her being hurt."

They watched in silence as the girl tipped her bowl and drained the last of her soup.

"How in the world did that tiny stomach hold so much?" Alice marveled.

"I think it's been empty all day. I wonder if she showed up this morning? I went straight to Portland from the meeting."

"Poor little thing."

They both stared at the child, and then Alice asked in an undertone, "Annie, what in the world do you plan to do with her?"

Annie sucked in a deep breath and let it out.

"I haven't even really thought past getting her warm, fed, and clean. I guess I should call the police."

"Probably you should."

"Yes."

Both women sighed in unison.

"So are you going to?" Alice said.

"Call the police? Of course. But look at her; she's tired. I think I'll bathe her and put her to bed. Then I'll call the authorities in the morning. Besides, however she got here, whatever has happened up to this point, she's been through enough for one day. I can at least give her a few hours of comfort and care."

Alice smiled at Annie and patted her arm. "I think you're right," she said. "I'll help you."

Annie gave her friend a grateful smile. "If you'd like to start a nice warm bath ... you can add some of that Mr. Bubble I bought to use for the twins ... it's in the guest bath upstairs. I'll see if I can find her something to wear."

Alice nodded. "I'm on it."

She patted the blond head as she passed on her way out the door. The little girl looked up and almost smiled. Her eyelids drooped, and it was easy to see she was nearly asleep in the chair. Annie picked her up.

"Honey, what's your name?"

The child shrugged.

"Don't you know your name?"

The girl blinked her large eyes.

"What does your mommy call you?"

The little girl shrugged.

"Do you know your mommy's name?"

Blink. Sigh. Thumb into mouth.

"Mommy," she whispered around the thumb and rested her head on Annie's shoulder.

Upstairs, Annie knelt in front of the girl and unwrapped the blanket from around her. She started to remove the faded, too small red sweat suit the girl wore when she saw a scrap of paper pinned to the ragged top.

"What's this?" She unclasped the safety pin and

unfolded a square of paper. She read it, and then said, "Alice? W-would you come h-here, please."

She stared at the note in her hand until Alice appeared in the doorway. "Annie! What's wrong?"

Wordlessly, Annie handed her the paper. The girl merely stood where she was and sucked her thumb.

Alice read the note aloud, "Dear Annie, Please take care of Noelle for me. I'll be back to get her." She looked up, eyes wide. "What?" She read the note again, silently this time. "Who wrote this?" She turned the paper over, looking for more writing. "Annie, where'd you get this?"

"It was pinned to her top, with this." She held up the safety pin. "We didn't see it earlier because we kept her bundled up in that blanket so she'd be warm."

The two women stared wordlessly at each other.

"What does it mean?" Alice whispered after a time.

Annie swallowed hard, turned her gaze to the sleepy child standing before her. The girl's eyelids drooped.

"I don't know," Annie said, "but I do know this child—Noelle—is about to fall asleep on her feet. I'm going to bathe her and put her to bed, and then I'll think about everything."

Once she had undressed and bathed the sleepy child in a warm, sudsy bath and washed her tangled hair, Annie dressed the girl in the smallest T-shirt she could find in her own dresser drawer. She carried her to the spare room she'd prepared for the twins, and then tucked her and the bedraggled teddy bear into the bed. For a while, Annie sat on the edge of the bed, stroking the silky, silvery hair, watching the little girl suck her thumb as she slept. How had this happened? Was it just a coincidence that Annie would find this needy little girl at a time when she needed someone to take care of? Was Noelle her gift from Stony Point's Santa? Even her name held a deeper meaning at this time of year.

She stopped herself, acknowledging that such pondering was foolish, if not wrong. This child was a person, not an inanimate trinket or toy.

"Where do you think she came from?" Alice whispered from the doorway, interrupting Annie's thoughts.

Annie shook her head.

"I wish I knew," she whispered back. "It's so odd, finding her here ...."

"I wonder if she's been kidnapped?"

Annie snapped her head around to look at her friend. "*Kidnapped?*"

The girl stirred. Annie turned back to her, but she still slept. She smoothed the blankets one last time and then leaned forward and kissed the thin pale cheek.

"Poor baby," she murmured. "Sleep well, little one."

Annie got up, turned on the bunny rabbit night light that she used when the twins visited, and snapped off the bedside lamp. She and Alice went back downstairs.

"What do you mean kidnapped?" she said the moment they reached the bottom step.

"As in *taken*, of course. Taken from her family."

"But she's in my house, Alice. *I* didn't take her."

"I don't mean *you*. I mean maybe someone abducted her and hid her here."

Annie sought words and found none. Alice had often come up with strange notions; this was no exception. Annie shook her head, trying to shake loose a reasonable response.

"Let's have some hot coffee," she said, finally. "This old house is still cold."

In the homey, comforting kitchen, she made fresh decaf and filled their cups.

"Honestly, I have to say your theory is a bit farfetched. Why in the world would someone steal a child and then stash her at my house? It's crazy."

Alice sipped her hot coffee, leaning forward. "Not really. I mean, think about it, Annie. Grey Gables isn't in a cookie-cutter neighborhood with neighbors really close. It's rather off to itself here. You have the woods and the pond to the sides. The beach isn't private; anyone can be out there."

"You mean maybe someone on the beach spotted this house and saw it as a safe haven?"

Alice nodded. "But temporarily. The kidnapper will return for Noelle."

"So, in your mind, the person who wrote that note abducted the little girl, strolled along the coastline of Maine, in the dead of winter, until they found my house and dropped her off ... for what reason? Safekeeping? Free babysitting? That idea is just too ridiculous for words."

Alice huffed at her.

"No, it isn't! Listen. This might have been in the works for a long time. Maybe someone chose your house back in the summer. You're friendly to everyone. When you take your walks along the beach, you probably talk to complete strangers, point to Grey Gables, and say 'I live right there.

Y'all come see me sometime.' That would be just like you, Annie. Just like you!"

Annie was already peeved at her friend for her lack of action on behalf of Sara earlier in the day. This unreasonable scenario rankled her like cold wind against chapped skin.

"My being friendly is part of who I am," she retorted. "I am not going to change just because I moved north. And for your information, I do *not* point out my house to complete strangers and invite them in. I'm not stupid, which is what this whole concocted story of yours is."

The two women glowered at each other.

"I'm just trying to help!" Alice snapped.

"Then don't come up with such a ridiculous theory! This is a serious situation, and we need clear heads and clear thinking."

Alice gulped the hot coffee and winced as it went down. She set the cup down with a definite *thunk* and put her fingers to her lips as tears sprang to her eyes. Annie got her a glass of cold water.

"Are you all right?" she asked. "Did you burn yourself?"

Alice shook her head and allowed the cold water to bathe her mouth and throat.

"I'm fine," she croaked. Then she sipped more water.

Annie watched, feeling irritated, guilty, sorry, deflated, and weary. She closed her eyes for a moment and rubbed her temples.

"I'm sorry for snapping at you. Let's start over," she said, opening her eyelids. "OK?"

Alice hesitated and then nodded. "I apologize too," she said. "I just said what popped into my head."

Alice often spoke before she thought, but Annie chose not to mention that little fact.

"I suppose your theory could be true," Annie said, "but I don't think it's too likely.

"Right. But *someone* put her in here."

"But who? And when? And how?" asked Annie.

"When I closed the rest of the windows for you, I saw the screen was off one of the windows in the living room," Alice said quietly. "I'm pretty sure that's how they got in."

"Oh," Annie said weakly. "Oh, my. Someone actually got into my house through one of those windows."

"Stella was right," Alice suggested.

"Yes." Something occurred to Annie. "But what if the windows had not been opened? Do you think the person would have left Noelle on the porch?"

"I hardly think so. She would have frozen to death. Probably they would have taken her somewhere else."

"Like the carriage house."

"Yes. Maybe they would have left her on my doorstep." Alice looked a little alarmed at the thought.

They sat silently, sipping coffee, thinking.

"Annie, you have to call the police," Alice said at last, in a voice so quiet Annie had to lean forward to hear her. "Whoever brought that little girl to Grey Gables is still out there somewhere."

"I know."

"They did not give you that child as a Christmas gift."

Annie met her friend's eyes. It seemed Alice knew her better than Annie had realized.

"I know that," Annie said, "but looking after her for a while is a bit of a gift—this year especially."

"Whoever left her here will be back."

Annie nodded. "Yes. That's what the note said."

"Annie," Alice said after a minute. "You need to call the police."

Rather than answer her directly, Annie said, "Listen to that wind, Alice. The storm is here."

"The police vehicles are able to get through snowstorms."

"We already talked about this. The poor little thing was exhausted, and now she's sound asleep."

"*Annie.*"

Right then, all Annie wanted to do was comfort and cuddle that little one sleeping upstairs. Once again, Alice seemed able to look into Annie's head and read her mind. She reached out and covered one of Annie's hands with one of her own. She squeezed gently, and her eyes brimmed with gentle understanding.

"She's not yours, Annie."

"I know that. But she's been given into my care by someone who's desperate—someone who trusts me to take care of her." She paused and then added, "That's exactly what I'm going to do."

That night, after Alice left and after Annie went to bed, Annie went over the events of the evening point by point. She thought of the pale, stoic face, thin arms and legs, and wispy white-blond hair. She remembered the sober expression in the large light-blue eyes. The child seemed to accept whatever life handed her, and Annie's motherly instincts told her Noelle had not been handed the best.

She heard a sound in the room and turned her head sharply. Noelle was padding across the room to her. The white T-shirt Annie had dressed her in nearly glowed in the darkness. She reached the bedside, thumb in mouth, bear clutched in one arm.

"Honey!" Annie said, sitting up in some alarm. She turned on the bedside lamp. "Why are you awake? Are you sick?"

The girl took her thumb from her mouth long enough to reach up with both arms. Annie hoisted her into the bed and felt her forehead.

"Not feverish. Do you feel OK?"

Noelle nodded.

"Are you scared?"

The little girl shook her head. "Sleep right dere," she said, pointing to the other side of the bed.

"You want to sleep in my bed tonight?"

Noelle nodded. She popped her thumb into her mouth and regarded Annie patiently. Annie folded back the covers, smiling.

"Crawl in here where it's warm."

Noelle clambered into place and laid down. Annie tucked the covers around her snugly.

"Is that better?" Annie asked.

The girl nodded.

"Are you sleepy?"

Noelle nodded again, her eyelids already drooping.

"Good. Me too. Let's get some sleep, huh?" Annie turned out the lamp and settled back down. A moment later, Noelle moved closer, her tiny body warm and sweet by Annie's side.

As Annie cuddled her, she pondered Alice's words. Call the police? Tell some authority figure who would take this little girl from Annie's safe, loving care and put her with a stranger? Put her in a home full of strangers who may or may not give her enough attention and care?

"No!" Annie whispered fiercely into the night. Someone had entrusted Noelle's care to her, and although she had no idea who had turned the child over to her, she was going to fulfill that trust.

— 44 —

*I*n the morning, Annie remembered the clothes she'd bought for John and Joanna a few years earlier—warm clothing needed in Maine they'd never need in Brookfield. Everything was too big, of course—the twins were only five-year-olds at the time—but Annie quickly altered by hand-stitching some underwear, a long-sleeved shirt and rompers. The socks fit high up on her spindly legs, but then she put Noelle's dingy, cloth sneakers back on the child's feet. She brushed the silky, fine hair into a ponytail, and then hand in hand, the two went into the kitchen for breakfast.

Noelle devoured a piece of toast, a steaming bowl of oatmeal with raisins, and a glass of milk.

"I do believe you look better already," she told the child. Indeed, the pale blue eyes shone and the thin cheeks had a bit of color.

When Noelle finished, she went upstairs with Annie into the spare room.

"I want to see if I can find any more clothes for you," Annie said. "Of course, I'll need to go to town to buy a few things, but let's see what we have here."

Noelle stood quietly beside her, teddy bear in one hand, thumb in her mouth. Annie knelt in front of the dresser and went through every drawer looking for anything she might have bought for the twins and forgotten about. She found two pairs of jeans, a couple of long-sleeve T-shirts, and two more pairs of socks. Always thinking ahead, she sometimes bought clothing or toys and games for her grandchildren, preparing for their visits, or more often, mailing the items to Texas with a note to remind them that she was thinking of them.

"I'm definitely going to have to go into town," she said finally.

"Town?" Noelle asked. "McDonald's?"

Annie raised her eyebrows. "McDonald's, eh? Well, I think you need more nutritious food than that for a while. Maybe in a week or two we'll get you a Happy Meal, OK?"

Noelle grinned around her thumb and nodded enthusiastically.

"In the meantime, I know Gram stored plenty of fabric in the attic. I can make you some clothes."

Noelle blinked, sucked, and smiled as if she understood every word.

It occurred to Annie she was looking at her little guest as long-term, and she told herself that was not the best way to handle the situation. At some point, whoever left her here would be returning.

Except I can't let her go back to a place where she obviously doesn't get enough food or the right kind of clothes. One thing she did not want to do was take the girl into Stony Point where curiosity and questions would abound. She'd have to reveal the presence of Noelle sooner or later, but the least she could do until that time was feed and clothe her properly.

Annie gathered the girl up in her arms and smothered the little face with kisses.

"Nanny," she said, pointing toward the front door.

Annie laughed in delight. "My name is Annie, but Nanny is close enough for a little girl who doesn't talk much."

"Nanny," Noelle said, sighing, still looking at the door.

"No, honey. We're not going outside now, but we'll go somewhere one of these days, I promise. Maybe even to Portland!"

Noelle sighed again and dropped her hand.

"Let's go upstairs," Annie said. "There's a regular treasure trove up there. I bet we can even find you some toys."

The attic was chilly and dim and smelled of the collected artifacts stored there. Annie grabbed an old quilt from a stack of them near the door and wrapped it about Noelle.

"Now, if I remember correctly," she said, "Gram had lots of fabric in that chest right over there." Noelle started to follow her, but Annie stopped her. "No, honey, stay right here. I'm afraid you may fall dragging around that quilt past all this stuff. Um ..." She looked around, spotted a stuffed toy elephant that had been hers in her childhood. She got it and handed it to the girl. "Here. His name is Binky-Boo, and he's been alone a long time. Play with him, sweetheart, right here, while I see if I can find some material."

Annie found a few yards of soft buttercup yellow flannel and a few lengths of darker, thicker fabric. She discarded some scratchy wools and latched onto some fluffy rose-pink fleece. The fabric was old. She didn't know how old, and she hoped it was sturdy enough to last. At least there was enough she could make several simple, warm outfits and pajamas for Noelle.

Downstairs, she put Christmas music on the CD player,

and then spent the morning in the dining room measuring Noelle and drawing patterns on discarded newspaper for pants, tops, and nightgowns.

"This is how my mother used to make clothes," she told the child. "We didn't always live near stores, so she made most of our clothes."

Noelle looked up from where she sat on the floor with the teddy bear and elephant, bouncing them along as if they were walking together. She smiled and then turned back to the toys. Annie paused a moment, her pencil poised just above the newspaper as she gazed at Noelle. The little girl was so quiet and well-behaved it was almost eerie.

A few minutes before noon, just as Annie was going into the kitchen to prepare lunch, Alice called.

"I made a large lunch, and it's ready right now," Alice said. "Why don't you and Noelle come over?"

Noelle was standing on her tiptoes, trying to see the tops of the counters, apparently looking for food.

"Meatloaf, mashed potatoes, peas, and hot rolls," Alice added, as if she could see into Annie's kitchen from the carriage house. "Comfort food."

"We'll be right over," Annie replied immediately, looking at Noelle's thin, eager face.

Annie grabbed a saltine from a canister and handed it to her. The girl crunched it happily.

"We're going to Alice's for a good, hot lunch," Annie said, "and that cracker will hold you until we get there. Now, let's go get bundled up."

The girl took a deep breath and stoically accepted being dressed in coat, gloves, scarf, hat, and snow boots.

If she did not have Noelle with her, Annie would have braved the snowy way like an old mountaineer through the trees between the two houses. But she refused to court any possible cold, germ, or virus getting hold of Noelle. Annie was glad she still had car seats from the twins' earlier visits, and putting one in the backseat of the Malibu took hardly any time at all. Annie strapped Noelle into the car seat, and then she drove the short distance to the carriage house.

Alice threw open her front door.

"Hey there, sweet thing," she said, kissing Noelle's cheek. She touched the tiny nose with the tip of her finger. "Are you hungry?"

Noelle nodded, and Annie removed the girl's mittens and unbuttoned her coat.

"This baby is going to be staying with me for a while," Annie said. She met Alice's eyes as she pulled the coat off the girl.

"You're sure that's the best thing to do?" asked Alice.

Annie handed Alice their wraps and then guided Noelle into the kitchen. The air smelled of homemade goodness.

"Let's get her settled in and then I'll tell you. OK?" Annie said.

Alice glanced at Noelle and nodded. "OK. By the way, I fixed her a booster seat of sorts with every pillow in the house."

The two women busily filled a small plate with tender meatloaf, fluffy mashed potatoes and brown gravy, baby peas, and hot yeast rolls.

"Do you have butter and jelly for the rolls?" Annie asked, glancing around for it.

"Annie," Alice said, gazing down at the plate, "I hope you don't expect her to clean her plate."

"It's OK if she doesn't," Annie said, smiling and stroking Noelle's hair as she picked up her spoon and dove into her meal. "But I think she's making up for lost time. Look at her go."

For a short time, they watched as Noelle happily shoveled in food. Then Annie drew Alice to the far side of the room and spoke to her in a lowered voice.

"I haven't called anyone about her, and I'm not going to for a while. Look at her, Alice. She needs some care, and I can give it to her."

They stared at the little girl.

"Does she cry for her mother?" Alice asked.

"No. Honestly, Alice, it's like she appeared from nowhere, thin, cold, and hungry, but detached from any root. It's just ... I don't know ... beyond strange. It's *weird*."

"Very strange."

"Exactly! If they find her family, I'm afraid they'd just hand her over like a bundle of clean laundry. At least I have the means and experience to care for a little one like her."

"They'd investigate first, Annie."

"But I'm not calling anyone yet. I can't make it any plainer than that."

Alice took in a deep breath and met Annie's eyes. "OK. I accept your decision. But don't you want to know where she came from and who left her here?"

"Of course I do! In spite of your somewhat wild notion that a stranger left her here, I can't help but think it's someone who knows me, or knows about me and realizes I can provide for the child. I feel confident that's why I have Noelle in my care right now. And like Stony Point's Santa, that person doesn't want to be identified."

Alice said nothing for a few moments. Finally, she said, "I just want you to be sure you're doing what you believe is the right thing before I tell you what I did."

"What'd you do, Alice?" Annie asked as a cold hand gripped her heart. "You haven't called Child Protective Services or anything, have you?"

"No, of course not! But this morning I did an extensive Internet search on my computer, looking at every database I could think of. I have found no mention or image of a little girl like Noelle being reported missing."

"That's a good thing, isn't it?" Annie said. "I mean, that means she's not been abducted or anything. Right?"

"It seems so to me."

"Well, then. That's all there is to it," Annie said. "I'm not going to agonize over where she came from, at least not for a while."

"Then I'm with you, and I'll do all I can to help." Alice smiled. "Let's join Noelle. I don't know about you, but that meatloaf is calling my name." She paused before adding, "Annie, what about that old man?"

"You mean the old man on the beach? I haven't forgotten him. I thought I'd check on him later, if you'll stay with Noelle."

Alice cleared her throat. "I don't mean that," she said. "I mean what about him and that little girl?"

Annie frowned. "What are you saying?"

"Think about it, Annie. He showed up on the beach, a stranger not far from you. You befriended him—"

"Well, I *tried* to befriend him. He seemed to want no part of friendship."

"Yes. But think about this. He shows up down there on the beach not far from Grey Gables. You say he's thin, dressed in ragged clothes, peculiar-acting, and you find out that he's living in some kind of old shack. Well, put two and two together."

Annie narrowed her eyes. "What are you getting at, Alice?"

"I'm just thinking." She tipped her head toward Noelle. "You were so generous with him. Maybe he brought her to you."

Annie's meatloaf went down hard. "You think the old man has something to do with Noelle? You think she's been with him all this time?"

Alice raised her eyebrows and her shoulders. "I don't know. But it adds up, doesn't it? Is it just a coincidence that they're both here at virtually the same time, in the same general state of being?"

"That surly old man and this sweet little child?" Annie made a sudden movement, as if trying to throw off such a notion. "Oh, Alice. No! Surely not."

But the more the idea clung to her thoughts, the more feasible it seemed. It would explain so much—except the reason for leaving a little girl with a stranger.

"Noelle?" Annie said. The child glanced at her and dug her spoon in what little mashed potatoes were left on her plate. "Honey, do you have a grandpa?"

Noelle blinked and put the potatoes in her mouth, but didn't say a word.

"She never says much, does she?" Alice said, refilling their coffee cups.

"Hardly a thing."

They ate quietly for a moment, each lost in thought.

"She has cleaned her plate, Annie. Shall I give her a little more?"

Annie studied the girl for a moment, noticing the heavy eyelids.

"No, I think she's full. I'll just put her to bed." She scooted away from the table and then dampened a thick paper towel at the sink. She washed off Noelle's hands and face, and then picked her up. "Is it OK to put her in the front bedroom?"

Alice nodded. "Tuck her under the comforter. It's soft and warm."

When Annie returned a couple of minutes later, she sat down and said, "She not only eats a lot, she sleeps a lot."

"Granted that I don't have a lot of experience with children, but isn't that rather unusual for a child her age? She's probably—how old—two or three? Don't children at this stage have so much energy you can't keep up with them?"

Annie nodded, picked up her coffee cup and sipped.

"Kids her age generally run around, whooping and hollering, getting into everything possible. They chatter ninety miles a minute and exhaust their caretakers. At least that was my experience with LeeAnn when she was little. When her twins came along, it was double the energy and chatter."

"I'll bet!" Alice said, laughing a little. She leaned forward and squeezed Annie's hand. "I know you miss your family, especially this year when you'll be without them for the holidays. I realize Noelle is filling that need for you right now. But I also know this: You have the best interests of that little girl at heart."

Annie fought back tears, shoving away her yearning to see LeeAnn, Herb, and the twins. She refused to substitute them with Noelle. The child needed to be loved for who she was, not for who she replaced. Annie cleared her throat and returned Alice's warm grip.

"Thank you for understanding. You're a true friend." They smiled at each other and then released each other's hands. "I'll help you get these dishes washed, and then if you'll watch Noelle for me, I'll walk down to the shack and talk to that old man. It's time for some answers."

Alice grinned.

"I love it when you get tough."

~ 12 ~

The cold wind off the water never ceased to take Annie by surprise. That day the wind bore teeth like a starving leopard, tearing into her throat and face, seeming to suck out her very breath. A weaker-willed person may have turned back to the warmth and safety of home, but Annie—who possessed strength of will and character—was on a mission. Not only would she never leave the old man to survive the winter without some form of intervention, she refused to let an abandoned child go to an unfit home or return to an unhealthy environment. She had to know if Noelle came from the stranger she'd cared for the last couple of weeks.

Gratefully, she stepped at last into the relative shelter of the cove. The wind still gnawed at her and the cold was bitter, but in the cove Annie didn't feel as though the elements would swallow her whole.

Ahead of her, the shack looked deserted. If a fire burned in the stove, the wind scattered its smoke before she could see it. Annie did not let the abandoned appearance deter her purpose, and she moved forward.

She knocked on the door, waited, and knocked again.

"Hello!" she shouted, knocking louder.

The door finally opened a couple of inches.

"Why are you here?" the old man said. "I told you not to come back."

"It's been a while since I was here, so I brought you a few groceries," she said, trying to keep her voice steady so as not to show the exasperation that she felt. "And actually, not that I need your gratitude, but saying 'thank you' would be good for your soul."

He said nothing.

"I want to ask you something."

He remained silent, but did not shut the door in her face.

"Did you leave me a 'little something' in my house yesterday?"

He blinked once, and his scowl deepened.

"You live in that old gray Victorian?"

"Yes."

"I didn't leave you anything. Good day."

He started to shut the door, but she thrust her foot across the threshold and grabbed the doorframe with one gloved hand.

"I'm talking about a little girl, about two or three years old. Did you leave a little girl at my house?"

His look of astonishment was almost comical, open-mouthed like a gasping fish.

"Lady," he said, after a moment, "I've thought all along you probably have a screw loose, and now I know for sure you do. Where would *I* get a little girl, and why would I leave one at *your* house?"

"I don't know, but someone did!" she blurted before she thought.

His mouth wagged again.

"Someone left a kid at your house? Why?"

"I don't know!" She all but stomped her foot, and to her

horror, felt tears sting her eyes. Where did they come from? She blinked rapidly. "I don't know why someone would leave a lethargic, underweight, poorly dressed little girl in my house while I was gone, but someone did. You are the only stranger I've come across near Grey Gables, so I just thought ...."

He held up one hand.

"You thought that I, being a stranger, left a child on your doorstep?" He laughed without humor, shaking his head. "It's almost Dickensian, isn't it?"

"I'm just trying to find where she came from," Annie said.

"Perhaps I'm a kidnapper, is that it?"

Annie's annoyance and consternation quickly flared into anger.

"I don't know you except as the sour, bitter old man I've been trying to help. For all I know you *are* a kidnapper! Or a bank robber. Maybe you run a dog-fighting ring."

He stared hard at her, apparently unmoved by the verbal attack.

"I take it that you resent that child," he said in a calm, reasonable voice that jarred her.

"What? No! Of course not. What a thing to say!"

"Then why are you out here, on a bitterly cold day with a storm brewing, asking a suspicious old man—an old man who may be a bank-robbing, animal-abusing kidnapper if he left an unhealthy, needy child on your doorstep? Why aren't you in your home taking care of her?"

Annie realized, with the weight of a falling house, the foolishness of going to his shack that day. His disposition would never have allowed him to be around a child in the first place, let alone try to find a good home for one.

"You're right," she said, backing away. "You'd never want, or even allow, a child around you. Children need love and want attention. They need to be taught manners and respect. They need *caretaking*. I'm sorry to have bothered you." She turned, walked a couple of steps, and then turned back. "Surly and ungrateful as you are, I refuse to leave you in need. Can I bring you anything?"

He stared at her through the small opening of the door for a long time. She watched as something crossed his features and settled in his eyes. He shook his head.

"I need nothing." He paused and then added, "Thank you."

He shut the door firmly, and Annie blinked in surprise. She wondered if that was the first time the man had said those two words in his entire life.

"You're welcome," she said to the closed door.

His two final words echoed in her mind all the way back to the carriage house.

*   *   *   *

When Annie got back to the carriage house, Alice was sitting in front of the TV watching *Judge Judy* and working on her cross-stitch. She muted the sound with the remote the instant Annie came in.

"You look absolutely frozen!" she cried, getting up. "I made some hot chocolate earlier. Let me pour your some."

Annie nodded gratefully. Her fingers were so stiff with

cold that she could barely remove her gloves and unwind the woolen crocheted scarf from her throat. Leaving her coat on and buttoned, she trailed Alice into the kitchen.

"Is Noelle still sleeping?"

"Still asleep, bless her heart," Alice said, pouring a huge white mug to the brim with steaming cocoa.

Annie accepted the mug and happily wrapped her fingers around the warmth.

"Mmm," she said, drinking. "Thank you. I needed that."

"Come into the living room and settle down," Alice said. "You can wrap that gorgeous russet afghan you made last year around your poor frozen body. I'll even turn up the heat."

"That sounds lovely," Annie agreed, returning to the living room. She all but gulped the hot chocolate. "I'll leave my coat on a bit longer too. I do believe my blood has frozen, maybe even the marrow of my bones."

Alice laughed with her. "I'm sure it feels that way, walking along the edge of the Atlantic Ocean, in Maine, on a blustery winter day."

"I'm a sucker for punishment, I guess, as often as I've done it in the last two weeks," Annie said. She settled into a small recliner. Before she could do more than take a couple of breaths, Alice had tucked the thick, soft afghan around her.

"Thank you," Annie said. She ran one hand over the stitches, fingering them gently. "I loved making this for you. The colors are so beautiful, and this shell pattern may be old-fashioned, but it's still one of my favorite patterns."

"Who says it's old-fashioned? Even if it is, it's gorgeous, and I love it!" Alice declared. "And because you made it for me, I love it even more."

The two of them smiled at each other. Annie's heart warmed in the presence of her friend. She and Alice sometimes had differences of opinions, but Annie doubted she could ever find a truer, more faithful friend in the world.

"Annie," she said, "before I forget it, I want to apologize for something."

"Oh?"

"Yes. It's why I came over to your house last night. At the meeting yesterday ... when the others were being less than kind about Sara Downs ...." Alice's looked down, her face flushing. "Well, I should have said something. I should have stood up for her like you did. Instead, I allowed myself to feel awkward, like a schoolgirl wanting to go with the popular crowd. I'm really sorry. It won't happen again." She looked up, meeting Annie's eyes. "Do you forgive me?"

Annie heard the words and knew the apology had been difficult for the strong-willed Alice. As irritated as she had been by her friend's lack of a backbone yesterday, Annie never doubted that Alice was tenderhearted or felt compassion for Sara.

"Of course I forgive you," she said warmly. "I know you, Alice MacFarlane, and you're a good woman."

Alice smiled, relief washing across her face.

"Thank you! Now, let me give you a refill before I sit down," she said, taking away the half-empty mug, "and when I come back, I want you to tell me what you found out from that old man."

The moment Alice returned with their cocoa, she sat on the sofa, drew her feet up under her, and said, "Shoot."

"He was surly as ever. In fact, I thought he wasn't even

going to come to the door, but I just kept knocking until he opened it."

Alice sipped her cocoa and lifted one eyebrow.

"Of course you did. And?"

"He had no idea what I was talking about. In fact, he accused me of not wanting Noelle."

"Huh?" Alice scowled. "What is he? Crazy?"

Annie shrugged.

"Well, what am I saying?" Alice continued. "Of course he is. Living in a shack on the beach in the winter up here? Yeah, he's nuts."

"Not nuts. Eccentric, I think, oddly turned for sure, but not nuts."

Alice made a face. "Trust you to stand up for him."

"I'm not standing up for him. You don't know him."

"And neither do you, Annie. What's his name? Where did he come from? Why is he here?"

Annie reluctantly acknowledged her friend had a point. She didn't know the old man at all. The only thing she knew was that he was elderly and alone in a place where even a young, healthy man should not stay during a harsh winter.

"What makes you think he had nothing to do with Noelle?"

"Because the shock on his face when I more or less accused him of leaving her here could not be duplicated by the best actor in the world. Besides, he's not the type to have a youngster around. Trust me on that. He's far too frail to be of a danger to anyone except himself, and right now he seems to be all right. I'll keep checking on him every day or two, and if he seems to be—"

"Oh, Annie, honestly! Sometimes you are too trusting for your own good."

"I don't think so," Annie said quietly. "Let's remember the Good Samaritan, or a dozen other examples from the Bible. Let's remember the verse: *For I was hungry and you gave me something to eat, I was thirsty and you gave me something to drink, I was a stranger and you invited me in.*"

Alice tilted her head sideways. "So speaks the daughter of missionaries. You know, you have a pure heart, Annie Dawson."

"That's nice of you to say," Annie said. "'To the pure all things are pure.' That's a scripture my parents often quoted to me."

They both sipped their hot chocolate in silence for a bit, and then Alice sat up straight so fast that she nearly sloshed some on herself and the sofa. "Oh! Oh, Annie! The latest from Stony Point's Santa!"

Annie was about to take a drink but paused with the cup to her lips. She wriggled with anticipation.

"What? Tell me!"

"Well, guess who was the recipient this morning?"

"I don't know," Annie said without even trying to guess. "Who?"

"Take a guess!"

"Goodness gracious, Alice, don't make me guess. *Who?* You?"

"Not me. Wally and Peggy Carson!"

A little thrill ran through Annie's blood. She set her mug on the coffee table.

"Tell me more! What did they get?"

"Annie, it's the best thing you can possibly imagine for that family. Santa paid off their mortgage!"

Annie's mouth fell open, and then she laughed with pure joy. There was not another couple in all of Stony Point she'd rather see receive such a generous gift.

"Peggy called me just a short time after you left," Alice said. "She was laughing and crying all at the same time. John Palmer had just called them from the bank with the news."

"I think that's the best news I've heard in a long time!"

"I agree," Alice said. "Just think how much easier life will be for them without that house payment hanging over their heads. Both of them work so hard."

"Yes! Oh, my goodness, I am just so happy for them!"

The two women sat grinning at each other.

"Let me ask you something," Annie said after a bit. "Do you still think I'm Santa? I mean, paying off that mortgage … you *know* I could not do that—right?"

Alice sighed, and tipping her head to one side slightly, studied Annie's face.

"I guess I'll have to give up that notion. If you had that kind of money, I have a feeling I would have known about it before now."

"Good! I'm glad you're finally seeing reason. And do me a favor. Make sure everyone else sees reason too."

Alice laughed at her. "I'll do my best. But I say whoever Santa is, I'm glad he or she favored Wally and Peggy."

"Amen to that!"

Alice glanced at Annie's cup. "Are you warm yet? Want some more cocoa?"

Annie shook her head. "I think I've had enough to keep me up for a few nights! Thank you, but no more. And yes, actually, I'm considerably warmer now. Warm enough maybe to shed this coat."

She unwrapped the afghan, unbuttoned the coat and removed it, shivering a bit as she shed its warmth.

"Who knows? Maybe one day I'll become acclimated to Maine winters."

"Maybe."

Noelle padded into the living room right then, rubbing at her eyes and yawning. She crawled up on Annie's lap and snuggled against her chest.

"Nanny," she said.

"Isn't that sweet, calling me Nanny instead of Annie?" Annie said, kissing the top of the girl's head. "Hello, sweetheart. Did you have a nice nap?"

The girl nodded.

Annie looked at Alice said teased, "What will she call you, I wonder? Malice?"

"Oh ha ha—very funny," Alice said, giggling. "She'll probably call me something like Beautiful Auntie Alice. Won't you, Noelle?"

The girl gave her a big-eyed look, popped her thumb in her mouth, and rested contentedly against Annie.

*   *   *   *

That afternoon, Annie cut out fabric and sewed two small, long-sleeve nighties. A cheery fire burned in the living room fireplace, and a rich stew simmered on the stove.

Noelle played with the bear and the elephant, and watched cartoons on television.

Shortly before twilight inked out the last of daylight, Annie heard something on the front porch. She was hand-stitching the hem on Noelle's second nightgown, but her needle stilled and she sat without moving, straining to hear. She might have dismissed the sound as her imagination, but Boots was staring at the front window, her eyes bright and her ears slightly laid back. Maybe the sound had been snow sliding from the rooftop, or a branch breaking in a nearby tree, but Annie was sure the noise had come from her front porch.

She put aside her sewing, got up, and stole quietly across the hall into the unlit dining room. Peeking outside with no light behind her, Annie narrowed her eyes, searching through the dimness and was rewarded to see movement. Someone hurried away, heading toward the coastal side of her property. She stared hard, and with a start recognized the black-and-red–plaid mackinaw that she had given to the old man from the beach.

— 13 —

Annie strained her eyes to be sure she saw what she thought she did. She could hardly believe it.

"Stay right there, Noelle," she said.

She grabbed up an earth-brown afghan, wrapped it around her shoulders and hurried outside.

Staring toward the figure that had crossed the road and now moved with speed farther from Grey Gables, Annie failed to see the bundle on her porch and tripped over it. Flailing like a windmill she struggled to keep from plummeting down the steps and managed to grab a post in the nick of time. She righted herself and caught her breath. Another glance to the east proved the old man was gone. There was no way Annie would chase after him, not without a coat and boots in the cold and snow—and she certainly wouldn't leave Noelle in the house by herself.

Annie's near-fall had torn open the package and caused some of the contents to spill out. She gathered the package and its scattered contents and went back into the house. Noelle stood a few steps away from the door, silent tears flowing down her chalk-white cheeks.

"Nanny!" she wailed.

In an instant, Annie understood the pallor, the tears, the fear in the child's eyes. Noelle had already been abandoned once; she obviously thought Annie had deserted her too. The items Annie held hit the floor as she rushed to Noelle.

"Oh, honey," she soothed the little girl. "Sweetheart, it's OK. Annie is here. Annie didn't leave you, and I *won't* leave you."

She gathered the little girl into her arms, and Noelle clung to her like a fresh green vine. The child pointed to the living room and again said, "Nanny."

Annie carried her into the other room, sat in the rocker, and put it in motion. The package, the old man, the frigid night ... all these faded in importance as she focused solely on comforting the little girl in her arms.

"Annie will never leave you alone, little one," she murmured.

Noelle stared at the window where the screen had been removed and her tears flowed. It seemed she silently cried for hours, and Annie's heart ached as she patiently rocked. She softly sang lullabies and Christmas carols until Noelle fell asleep against her. Even then, Annie held her, protecting and comforting, until she was sure the child was deeply asleep. Annie carried her upstairs, put her in one of the new nighties and tucked her in, all without the child waking up. She sat on the edge of the bed for a time, remembering nights long ago when she'd put her own daughter to bed and watched over her while she slept. With a tender smile, she planted a soft kiss on Noelle's warm cheek, turned on the night light and went downstairs.

Just a couple of feet inside the front door lay the contents of the package she'd found on the front porch. The first thing her gaze landed on was an apple-green downy snowsuit in a size small enough to fit Noelle. She picked it up, stared at it and then looked to see what else was there: tiny boots, some earmuffs, a dress coat, a pair of sturdy sneakers, shiny black Mary Jane shoes, tights, a baby doll and a stuffed white bear. As Annie examined the virtual treasure trove of little girl's clothing, she felt her eyes get wider and wider.

Her gaze fell on a small envelope almost hidden by the package wrappings. White and about five inches square, it was sealed. Annie broke the seal and removed a note written in a neat, upright script.

"An early Merry Christmas, from Stony Point's Santa," she read aloud. She stared at the note and then flipped it over. She picked up the discarded envelope. Checking for anything written on it, and finding nothing on the outside, she looked inside. It had held the note and nothing more.

"My goodness," she said, faintly, sitting flat on the floor. Almost everything Noelle would need immediately was contained in that anonymous gift. "My goodness," she repeated.

Her thoughts raced, a thousand ideas flowing along what seemed, at the moment, an endless stream of possibilities. Had Alice made this generous gesture? After all, she was the only one who knew about Noelle; maybe she thought being a Secret Santa would be fun.

A sudden idea popped into Annie's mind and she scrambled to her feet. Upstairs from a small keepsake box on her dresser, she plucked out the note that had been attached to Noelle's sweatshirt. She compared the handwriting, confirming there was nothing in the first note that looked remotely like the writing in the other one.

Only one possibility remained.

You know who brought these gifts, Annie, she thought. *You saw him hurrying away.*

"Wouldn't everyone in town be astonished to know that Stony Point's Santa is not the jolly old St. Nick they all would expect him to be?" she whispered.

She carefully refolded the note and put it back with her other keepsakes. She carried the note from Santa downstairs with her.

Annie carefully gathered all the gifts and carried them into the living room. She looked at every item, noting its quality, its brand-spanking newness. These things were not inexpensive. In fact, it seemed no expense had been spared to provide warmth and happiness for that little girl upstairs.

She knew where the gifts came from; in fact, how could she deny what her own eyes had seen? But the logical part of her brain simply could not grasp the fact that a crotchety old recluse who dressed in virtual rags and lived in a falling-down shack was remotely interested in Christmas, giving gifts, or helping anyone in need. Why on earth had that old man decided to be Stony Point's Santa? And how was it that he had the means to be so generous?

"It does not compute," she muttered in a robotic monotone, rubbing her temples.

She reached for the telephone, but then she paused. Her first instinct had been to call LeeAnn and see what she might have to say. But on second thought, LeeAnn would want to know more about Noelle, and doubtless she would attempt to persuade Annie to turn the child over to Child Protective Services. A disagreement between them would probably erupt, and Annie refused to have a falling out with her daughter, particularly this close to Christmas.

Instead of calling LeeAnn, she dialed the number for the carriage house. It rang so many times, Annie was on the verge of hanging up when Alice finally answered.

"Hello?" Her friend's voice was breathless, and she sounded distracted.

"Did I catch you at a bad time?"

"Oh, Annie! God bless you! No, you called at the right time, because I was going to call you in just a minute if I could not get my furnace to light."

"Your furnace is out?"

"Yes. It went out about an hour ago, and I've been trying like mad to start it again. Honestly, I'm at my wit's end and freezing to death! What do I know about furnaces?"

"Have you called anyone?"

"Have I? Yes! But everyone I've called is out on calls elsewhere. Stony Point doesn't have a plethora of furnace repairmen, though apparently we should!"

"You know you're more than welcome to stay with me," Annie said with considerable warmth. Right then, with her most recent discovery, she couldn't wait to share the news and her speculations with Alice.

There was the smallest silence; then Alice sniffled and said, "Thank you. I would love to stay in Grey Gables with you. Oh, Annie, you're going to get *sick* of me."

"What a thing to say to your best friend. Pack a bag and come over."

"Maybe I should just leave an entire supply of necessities at Grey Gables since it looks like I'll be staying there so much."

Annie laughed. "That's fine. Stay as long as you want. Oh, and when you get here, I have something to show you!"

A few minutes later, when she opened the door to let her friend inside, Annie discovered more than Alice waiting for admittance. Ian Butler stood next to Alice, a big smile on his face.

"Ian!" Annie said, at once happy and dismayed to see him. "What a surprise!"

"We met coming up the steps," Alice said with false brightness. Her eyes signaled alarm as she stomped snow from her boots and leggings. Annie swallowed down her own urge to panic. She had neglected to consider unexpected visitors while Noelle was in the house, and turning Ian away from her door ... how could she justify that?

"Hi, Annie." He held up a large flat box. "I brought pizza from Sal's Pizzeria. I know it's your favorite pizza place in town. Hope you like it deluxe, because I had him make it that way."

In spite of Ian's untimely arrival, Annie could not deny the pizza he carried had a most enticing aroma of garlic, warm cheese, spicy meat, and tomatoes.

"How nice. My goodness. How nice of you to drop in, Ian," Annie said, sputtering and stammering a little. "And to bring pizza. It's been a while since I've had any food—er, I mean, pizza."

Ian flashed a look back and forth between the two women, and then he lifted one eyebrow.

"What's up, ladies?" he asked. "You both look like you've been caught sneaking cookies."

Annie and Alice looked at each other, trying to

communicate without speaking. How were they going to keep secret the presence of a little girl? Houses seemed to change somehow when children were there. *Maybe,* Annie thought, *Noelle will sleep, and Ian will never know she's here until the time is right.*

But she knew that, at some point, Ian would find out about the girl. How would he feel if he learned Annie kept her a secret from him? Would he feel betrayed? Angry? After all, the two of them were almost an item. *Almost,* she underscored in her mind.

"Come in, come in!" she said with more buoyancy than intended.

She and Alice exchanged another "What'll we do?" glance as Alice crossed the threshold.

"Let's go to the kitchen," Annie said as she shut the door behind them. "I'm sure the pizza has cooled off in that cold air. I'll just put it in the oven to warm. Here, let me take your coats."

Ian handed Annie the pizza box as he peeled off his black wool overcoat and then exchanged the coat for the pizza. He had a slight frown.

"I still think something is going on here," he said.

Alice handed Annie her coat and giggled. It lacked the genuineness of her usual happy laugh. She took Ian's arm and said, "Let's go put this pizza in the oven and make something hot to drink while Annie hangs up our coats. I'm freezing, aren't you?" She kept chattering nervously as she escorted him to the kitchen. "You know, Ian, since my furnace isn't working, I left my water dripping and the cabinet doors under the sink in the kitchen and bathroom open, and space heaters on facing them. Do you think that will keep my water pipes from freezing? All I need is a burst pipe!"

Annie stood where she was for a moment, holding their wraps and thinking. Thank goodness, Alice could think fast and brought up a new topic to distract Ian from speculating about secrets and suspicious behaviors. But she wondered if maybe she should tell him about Noelle. As much as she liked and respected him, did she trust him to keep her secret? Would he understand her commitment to the child, or would he think she should hand Noelle over to authorities? Would he pressure her to let go?

There was no real answer, of course, because there was no way of knowing what the man would do until he was faced with the situation. If it were up to Annie, she wouldn't have to face the situation either, but it had happened, and she was doing what she felt was the right thing.

Annie glanced up the darkened staircase. Noelle had been traumatized earlier when Annie ran out onto the porch. It was obvious the child was afraid she would be abandoned again. When Annie had calmed her and she finally slept, the sleep had been deep and hard-won. More than likely, she would not wake up until morning.

Annie hung Ian and Alice's coats in the hall closet. A single glance at the pile of clothes and toys on the living room sofa would tell anyone they were for a small child, and that would raise questions.

I'll just keep Ian in the kitchen until he decides to go home, she thought as she turned off the light in the living room.

When she entered the kitchen, the metal of the cold oven popped as the heating element warmed it up. Ian had arranged the pizza on a round pizza pan, and Alice was adding some spices to a potful of apple cider. The cinnamon, nutmeg and other spices in the cider released a fragrance into the air that warmed body and soul.

Ian glanced up.

"How are things, Annie?" he asked. Did his eyes probe hers with that direct gaze, or was he just being his usual friendly self?

"Fine, Ian," she said. "Wonderful, if fact. Isn't the snow lovely in the moonlight?"

He nodded and smiled. "It is. And there's more where that came from. You know, we Mainers like our snow a little on the heavy and frequent side; otherwise, it just doesn't seem like winter."

"I'm sure that's true enough." She glanced at Alice who seemed intent on stirring the mulled cider. "That smells *so* good, Alice."

"When I mixed these spices and gave you this bottle of them a couple of weeks ago," Alice said, shaking it significantly toward Annie, "I was hoping you'd make use of it."

"I have! Look, you can tell I have."

Alice held up the decorative shaker bottle and eyed the level of the rusty-color contents.

"Hmm. Maybe a few sprinkles."

Annie made a face and turned to Ian.

"Honestly, have you ever seen such a pushy friend in all your life?" she asked him.

He laughed, shooting a look at Alice and the shaker she still held.

"If you want to push any food stuffs toward me, Alice,

push away. Annie, you don't know a good thing when it lives next door to you!"

"Well said!" Alice said with a grin. "Y'see? Ian appreciates me."

Annie burst out laughing. It felt so good to have friends in her kitchen. The yuletide smell of spiced cider in the air, the warmth of the oven coming forth as Ian opened the door to set the pizza inside—all of it wrapped around her like a comfortable blanket.

"Y'all have a seat at the table, and I'll get plates and cups. And napkins. We mustn't have pizza without napkins!" She got a box of paper dinner napkins from the pantry. "Shall I put out forks too?"

"No!" Ian and Alice said in unison.

"What's the fun in eating pizza if you use a fork?" Ian said.

"That's right!" Alice nodded her head vigorously.

"All right," Annie said with a laugh, setting plates and napkins on the table. "But definitely napkins."

"I never need a napkin, dahling," Alice announced, waving one hand with the exaggerated gesture of a *prima donna*. "I never spill."

"Neither do I," Ian agreed with equal drama.

"I'm absolutely perfect," she said. "Aren't you, Ian?"

"Indubitably," he replied with a bad British accent.

Annie gave them a look of mock scorn.

"Of course you are. Both of you." She sat down and cleared her throat with the prissiness she'd learned from one of her high school English teachers. "Now back to the real world. It's hard to believe Christmas is just a couple of weeks away, isn't it? My, hasn't the year gone fast?"

"The older you get, the faster it goes," Ian agreed.

"And when you keep busy," Alice added, "it just flies."

"So, Annie," Ian said, his head tilted slightly to the side, "without your family coming to Stony Point, have you decided what you're going to do on Christmas Day?"

"Why, I'll stay right here with—" She broke off abruptly realizing she'd been about to say she would stay right there with Noelle. "—with Alice, of course!"

Alice gave her a wide-eyed look, and then turned a bright smile to Ian, "Of course! We're going to have Christmas right here in Grey Gables."

Ian shifted his gaze from face to face a few times.

"I see."

An uncomfortable silence fell over the trio until Annie said, "Alice, I think the cider is probably ready to pour, isn't it?"

"Oh! Yes! I'm sure! Let me just pour some for everyone ..." Alice nearly knocked her chair over in her hurry to stand.

Annie glanced at Ian. She had a strong inkling that he had planned to ask her to spend Christmas Day with him. The very notion filled her with anxiety, because she never liked deceit and secretive behavior. And yet ... a look at his bewildered, almost hurt expression struck her heart.

He was probably waiting for an invitation from her to come to Grey Gables.

"Let me check that pizza," she said, too loudly and with too much enthusiasm.

"Annie. Alice." Ian's eyes were narrowed. "What is going on here?"

Annie opened the oven door. Fragrant heat puffed outward, onto her face, then filled the kitchen. With great deliberation, Annie pulled on an over mitt and removed the pizza.

"Ummm," she said, "this looks and smells wonderful, Ian. Thank you so much for stopping by on such a cold night."

"Annie?" he said with an odd tone in his voice. She busied herself by carefully removing a large dripping with cheese and laying it gingerly on his plate.

"*Annie,*" Alice echoed, only her voice carried something different.

Annie raised her head and saw that both their attention was directed to the kitchen doorway.

"Hungry!" piped a small voice. In her yellow nightie and white socks, teddy bear under one arm, Noelle padded into the room. Her pale eyes scanned the scene for food and brightened as she saw the pizza.

Ian was looking at the girl as if he'd never seen a child before.

— 14 —

"Noelle!" Annie got to her feet and rushed to the girl. "Honey, why are you out of bed? Oh, you're little feet are going to freeze on this cold floor!"

She swept the child up and carried her into the kitchen, rubbing the chilly feet with one hand. Noelle giggled sleepily and wriggled her toes, and then she pointed to the pizza.

"Hungry!"

Annie kissed one cheek. "You're always hungry. Here, Alice, cuddle her up so she doesn't get cold." She deposited Noelle on Alice's lap. "I'll get an afghan and then some pizza."

"I can do that," Ian volunteered. He picked up a plate and selected a small slice.

Annie hurried into the living room, returning a few moments later with a soft rose-pink afghan. Annie and Alice watched Ian cut a slice into child-sized bites, exchanging glances. Annie busied herself with tucking the cover around Noelle's thin body.

"I'll pour her a glass of milk," Annie said. "In fact, I'll warm it up for her. Maybe it will help her sleep."

"I've heard warm milk is good for that," Alice said, still watching Ian cut up the food.

When he finished, he pushed the plate toward Noelle and smiled at her. She pressed back against Alice, her eyes large and serious, and her gaze fixed steadily on Ian. Her thumb found its way into her mouth. She ignored the food on her plate to watch him.

"Hi there," he said, reaching out to touch her hand. She shrank back, and Ian moved his hand. "I'm sorry. I think I frightened her."

Annie heated a cup of milk in small pan and gave him a gentle smile.

"It's not you, Ian. There must be another reason she reacted to you this way."

Alice reached over and patted his forearm reassuringly.

"We've no idea what her background is. Maybe someone who resembled you has hurt her, or maybe she is just scared of men."

He dragged his eyes from the child and looked at Alice. "What do you mean?"

"Well … um, that is …" She glanced at Annie.

"We don't know who Noelle is," Annie blurted out, knowing circumstances now dictated how she handled this situation with Ian.

A strange expression settled on his face.

"I beg your pardon?"

Noelle wriggled, and Annie poured the milk. She took the girl from Alice and sat down at the table. She pulled Noelle's plate toward them. The girl looked at the pizza, but didn't reach for it. Annie plucked up a piece and handed it to her.

"I found her," she told Ian.

Both his eyebrows went up.

"Say that again, Annie."

She squared her shoulders and cleared her throat.

"I said, I found her—here at Grey Gables." Then she told him the entire story, leaving out nothing except the part about the old man on the beach.

When she finished, Ian sat silently, watching as she handed the bites of pizza to Noelle, and then held the cup to her lips. The adults had yet to eat their own food.

He took a deep breath, opened his mouth as if to speak but then exhaled and said nothing.

"Ian?" Annie said. "Please ... tell us what you're thinking."

He spread his hands and shook his head. "I don't know what to say, Annie. At least now I know why you and Alice were acting like you'd robbed a bank and were trying to hide the stash when I showed up." His eyes went to Noelle. "And you have absolutely no idea who she belongs to?"

"None."

"Not a clue," Alice said, "except for that note pinned to her clothes."

"Hmm." Ian rested both elbows on the table and inter-locked his fingers. He rested his lips and chin against his clasped hands. "Hmm." Annie figured this was his thinking pose, familiar and well used during his days supervising the affairs of the town.

Annie felt Noelle grow heavier in her arms. She glanced down and saw the girl was almost asleep again.

Ian stared at her a bit longer and then said, "What are you going to do, Annie? About her?"

"I'm going to take care of her, of course. Feed her, make sure she's warm and safe."

"Hmm."

She shifted Noelle's weight.

"Actually, Noelle is much better off with Annie!" Alice said, somewhat defensively.

Ian raised one eyebrow.

"I'm sure she is. Annie would never break into someone's house and leave a child there. Plus, that little girl looks like she's missed a few meals."

"She eats enough for three grown men!" Alice declared.

Again silence spread among them, broken only by the whispery sound of Noelle's gentle breathing.

"You're going to get in touch with the right people, aren't you?" he asked at last. It was the question Annie dreaded the most, the subject that had brought her and Alice to a quarrel. She did not want to argue with Ian too.

"I suppose I must—at some point. But not for a while."

"But—"

"This child was given into my keeping. I will care for her until the right time comes for me to make other arrangements."

Ian took in another deep breath and held her gaze.

"And what constitutes 'the right time'?"

She stood, Noelle now a dead weight in her arms.

"I'm not sure, Ian, but I suspect I'll know it with extreme certainty when it gets here. And I won't be talked into doing something that goes against my heart and soul." She softened her tone with a smile. "I'm sure you understand. And now, I'll tuck this child back into bed, and when I come back, we'll enjoy that pizza. Alice, maybe you ought to stick it back in the oven. It's probably cold by now."

As she left the room, she heard Alice say, "She means it,

Ian. She's like a mother bear."

When Annie returned a bit later, the pizza was warm, and three large white mugs brimmed with spiced cider.

"So, Annie," Ian said as she seated herself, "am I invited to spend Christmas Day with you, Alice, and Noelle, or must I malinger at home, alone on the holiday?"

Alice grinned, and Annie felt relief sweep through her. Whether it had been her own words or something Alice might have said that convinced Ian to keep her secret, she didn't know. At that point, she didn't care, as long as he held her confidence about Noelle.

"Absolutely!" she said. "I'm going to fix a big family-style dinner, and it just wouldn't be complete without you." She reached for a slice of pizza. "This may have turned cold two or three times in the last hour or so and been warmed over, but it smells good, looks good, and I'm sure it tastes great." She bit into the thin, firm crust, spicy sauce, and soft layer of cheese. "Umm. Oh, my goodness. Sal knows how to make a pizza."

"That he does. I watched him make this, tossing the dough in the air, smiling and singing *New York, New York* at the top of his lungs. He's from New York City, you know."

"Well, their loss is our gain."

They consumed the pizza and talked lightly about the weather, the town, and the latest movie showing at the theater.

"You know," Ian said, while he munched on his third slice, "this Stony Point secret Santa business seems to be spreading."

Annie stopped chewing and looked at him with interest. There was no way he knew yet about the gifts left on her front porch for Noelle, and Annie wasn't going to mention them, not for a while anyway. First she planned to chase down her undeniable lead and see if Stony Point's Santa lived in a shack on the beach not far from where they now sat. And after that she'd share the news of Noelle's gifts.

"Who received what this time?" Alice said.

"Not so much of someone receiving a gift from an unknown benefactor this time, but Bennett Woods called me today. He and his family have decided to deed that portion of land they own on the west side of town for a community garden. Not only that, he said Gil Landry has agreed to plow sections for each member, and Mike Malone will donate tomato seedlings to the first twenty-five gardeners who choose to participate. I know it's a long way until gardening season, but what generous donations to our town! I tell you, ladies, this secret Santa has opened up a door of giving that I wish would spread to the whole world."

"So do I!" both women said in unison, fervently.

Annie wondered what Alice or Ian would say if they knew a crotchety old man started this wave of generosity. They'd probably think she was crazy for having such notions.

*   *   *   *

The next morning, Annie stood in the living room, gazing at the frigid Atlantic water while she sipped her morning coffee. The house was silent except for the invading sound of wind.

"Good morning, neighbor," Alice said, shuffling into the living room in fuzzy slippers and a robe as thick as a bearskin. "I smell coffee."

Annie smiled. "Good morning. You smell a whole potful. Are you ready for breakfast?"

Alice waved one hand. "Just some coffee. Ask me about breakfast after I wake up." She yawned and shuffled out again, heading toward the kitchen. Annie grinned, watching her leave. As much as she hated that her friend's heating system was out, Alice's presence in Grey Gables pleased her. Having Noelle and Alice in the house was like being with family.

"How about if I make some waffles?" Alice asked when she returned with her coffee. She stood by Annie and looked at the frozen landscape. "Waffles are one of my specialties."

Annie smiled at her. "All your baking and cooking is special, as far as I'm concerned."

Alice returned the smile and sipped her hot coffee.

"Beautiful out there, isn't it?" she said. "Everything looks so clean, so unspoiled."

"Winter has its own style of beauty," Annie agreed. "Of course, I love spring."

Alice sipped again. "I know. But that's a long way off."

They stood in silence a bit longer, and then Annie spoke her thoughts aloud. "I wonder if Noelle will still be here in the spring."

"You aren't planning to keep her a secret for that long, surely."

Annie hesitated, but then she agreed. "No. I'll need to let someone know."

"If I were you, I'd see about taking those classes to be a foster parent. That way, maybe she can stay with you."

"I've been thinking about that myself. I looked online at the requirements for being a foster parent, and I believe after the holidays, I'll go to the Department of Health and Human Services office and get the paperwork started."

Alice turned from the window and settled down in an armchair. "Annie, when did you get all that?"

Annie turned and saw her friend's gaze fastened on the pile of gifts from Stony Point's Santa.

"Actually, I found it. Last night, on the porch."

Alice lifted both eyebrows. "What?" she asked.

"Hang on," Annie said, putting down her cup. "I'll show you something." She hurried upstairs and took the note that had accompanied the package from the dresser where she'd laid it last night. Downstairs again, she handed it to Alice. "Here. Take a look at this."

Alice read it and then shrieked, "Are you kidding me?"

"Shhh! Don't wake Noelle!"

Alice clapped one hand over her mouth for two seconds and then stage-whispered, "This is so great, Annie! Wow!"

Alice examined each item of clothing and every toy, excitedly but silently bobbing in admiration or giggling at the "cute factor."

"Look at these itty-bitty boots! Aren't they the sweetest things you've ever seen—" Suddenly she broke off. "But Annie! How in the world did anyone know about Noelle being here ..." She paused for a second, and then said, "*Ian!* He's the only person other than you and me who knows about her." Alice's blue eyes sparkled so lively that they looked like diamonds. "Ian Butler is Stony Point's Santa. Oh, Annie, he didn't so much as flicker an eyelash to give himself away!"

"That's because Ian Butler is *not* Stony Point's Santa," said Annie confidently.

"Of course he is. He's the only other one who knows about her ... well, except for whoever left her here, of course, and whoever left her here could not possibly be a generous, anonymous gift-giver. Someone like that would never leave a child with a stranger."

"These clothes were left on the porch before you and Ian showed up."

A frown creased Alice's pretty face. "Then who?"

"You're forgetting who I talked to the other day, accusing him of leaving her with me."

Alice's expression changed to one of disbelief.

"The old man on the beach! *The old man on the beach?*" She spoke as if saying the words often enough would fit together every piece in the puzzle. *"Really?* No, Annie. From what you've told me, he's a step or two down from Ebenezer Scrooge. There is no way some surly, antisocial old geezer is going out and buying fluffy little trinkets and outfits for a toddler. No way."

"I hear you, Alice. I understand what you're saying, but yesterday at dusk, before you and Ian showed up, I heard something out on the porch. It took me a few seconds to get up and go outside, but when I did, I saw him just as he disappeared across the road, going toward the beach."

Alice frowned. "About dusk you say? That means it was dark—"

"Almost dark."

"Really too dark for you to actually recognize anyone, I imagine."

"But I saw his coat. It was that red-and-black–plaid mackinaw I gave him."

"Annie, for goodness' sake. There are probably 300 coats just like that in Stony Point. In fact, I bet nearly every house in the entire state of Maine has a red-and-black–plaid mackinaw in it. They aren't unique."

"But the person wearing it went across the road in the direction of the beach."

"So? If whoever it was saw you coming out the door, they were probably trying to duck out of sight."

"Even so, I just have a feeling it's him."

Alice crimped her mouth and gave Annie a level stare.

"I'm sorry if you disagree, Alice, but it's something I feel deep inside."

Alice plucked at the snowsuit on her lap, her eyes on the snowman stitched on the front of it.

"OK, Annie. I trust your instincts most of the time, so I see no reason to change now." She looked up, smiled, and added, "Even when your ideas fly in the face of logic."

"I know it doesn't make sense to you. It doesn't make sense to me either." Annie stared at her friend over the rim of the cup as she drank. "You know," she continued thoughtfully, "this has been the oddest holiday season ever. So many questions and no real answers."

Alice nodded and set aside the snowsuit.

"I agree. But Ian was right. Whoever this mysterious Santa Claus is, he or she has really started something in our town. Look at all the gifts and services that have been given, free of charge, that have nothing to do with our Santa." She began to tick them off on her fingers.

"Mary Beth received that refrigerator, and then you and Stella give her more things to make the break room comfortable. I found out that someone paid to have the snow plowed off my driveway—and yours—the other day. Bennett Woods donated land for a community garden."

Annie sat up so suddenly that she spilled her coffee. "Oh, my goodness!" she cried. "Oh, my goodness! All this excitement with Noelle completely chased Sara's bookmarks out of my mind. I have a large order for them from a couple of places in Portland, and they want them ASAP. I need to take the order to her right now."

"You know," Alice said thoughtfully, "we were talking about how people seem to be in the Christmas spirit so much this year ... well, I'd like to give Sara Downs some new clothes. Do you think she'd be OK with that, or do you think she'd be offended?"

Annie shook her head. "I doubt she'd be offended. Ask her."

"Or," Alice said, her eyes lighting up with a new idea, "I could leave them anonymously for her at the Atlantic Jewel or at The Cup & Saucer. That way, she'll be a recipient of gifts from an unknown person just like the others."

Annie felt her smile bloom at the idea. "I like that notion. I'll help!"

Alice clapped her hands. "Good!"

"While I go upstairs and change, why don't you write up a list. Then if you stay here with Noelle, I'll stop at Dress to Impress and pick them up while I'm in town," Annie said. "Being a secret Santa is fun!"

Alice had to agree.

~ 15 ~

Annie's first stop was at Dress to Impress, and she bought everything from petite-size nightgowns to jeans to a party dress. She purchased work shoes, sneakers, and dress shoes, and prayed they'd fit. The clerk who helped was no one Annie recognized, and for that she was thankful. She did not want word to get out that she was buying clothes that obviously were not for her.

Annie's next stop was the Atlantic Jewel. She entered the little office that looked every bit as dismal as she expected, with its dingy tan paint and cheap faded pictures of ships on the walls. It stank of stale cigarette smoke, but as Annie glanced around for the manager, she noticed the front desk was spotlessly clean, the floor swept, and the windows shining.

A balding middle-aged man—with the careworn expression of someone who does more than he has time for—came from a room behind the desk.

"Help you?" he asked.

"I'm looking for Sara Downs."

"Ah, Sara." He nodded. "She's working over at The Cup & Saucer today." He frowned and gave Annie a sharp look. "She in some kind of trouble? I don't want any problems here."

"No, no trouble at all. I'm her friend, Annie Dawson."

He nodded again. "I know who you are. Grey Gables,

right? Yeah, I've heard about you." He held up both hands as though stalling a protest and gave her a gap-toothed smile. "All good, of course. Not a bad word have I heard."

Annie returned his smile. "That's nice to know."

He sobered quickly. "What d'ya need Sara for?"

She hesitated a moment and asked, "If I were to bring some things by here for her—gifts, that is—would you please see that she gets them, but not tell her where they came from?"

His eyes lit up. "I heard rumors that you might be the secret Santa who has been giving away gifts right and left."

"And a *rumor* is all it is," she said. "I'm happy to help when I can, and I would love to be able to do the kind of giving that's been done lately, but I'm not Stony Point's Santa. A friend of mine and I have gone together and got some things for Sara, and well, we didn't want to embarrass her, so we thought we'd give them to her anonymously."

He nodded enthusiastically. "I see. Well, I think that's a fine idea you and your friend had. Sara is a nice lady. She's quiet and clean, and I don't usually have a bit of trouble out of her. But the other day ...."

"The other day?" Annie asked.

"I don't know what was going on, but there was quite a ruckus outside her room—shouting and such. Before I could get out there to see what was happening someone jumped in a car and sped off. I went to her room and tried to talk to Sara, but she wouldn't talk. She barely opened the door to me. Only time I ever had any problem with her." He paused then added, "I can't have that kind of trouble here. This place ain't the Hilton, and it attracts some of the seedier sort, but I make it plain: You cause problems, you're outta here. But Sara—I like her. I don't want her to go."

Annie noted the soft expression in his eyes when he talked about the woman. Whether Sara knew it or not, she had an admirer and champion in this fellow. "I have the gifts for her out in the car. May I bring them in here, and will you see that she gets them?"

"I will."

"Thank you!" She reached out her hand to shake his. "Thank you so much!"

"It pleases me to see that lady smile. I hope I get to watch her open those gifts, but she's mighty private. By the way, I'm Aaron Webster."

"Thank you, Mr. Webster. I'll run out, bring everything in and give you the gift receipt. If anything doesn't fit, please tell Sara she can exchange it at Dress to Impress. And remember, not a word that I brought the gifts here."

*   *   *   *

Annie's third stop was The Cup & Saucer. Few diners sat at tables during the mid-afternoon, and the owner, Jeff, sat alone at a booth closest to the kitchen.

"Hi, Jeff," said Annie, greeting him with a smile.

Jeff looked up, slightly distracted, but when he saw her his face cleared and he smiled. "Well, hello, Annie. Have a seat." He indicated the seat across from him, removed his reading glasses and slid a few papers to the side. "How are you? Would you like some coffee?"

Annie sat down.

"Thank you, no. I can only stay a minute or two. I'm do-ing great," she said. "Just busy preparing for Christmas, of course. How's your family?"

"Doing well. My sister will be here for Christmas. I haven't seen her in a couple of years."

His words pricked her heart a little, reminding Annie that her own family would be absent during the holiday season.

"That's wonderful. I hope you enjoy her visit."

"I'm sure I will. We always have a good time together, but she lives in San Diego, so we have the entire country between us and don't get to see each other very often."

Annie glanced around and saw one waitress filling salt shakers and another pouring coffee for a couple of men across the room. Peggy was nowhere to be seen, and she wondered briefly if Peggy would quit her job now that the mortgage on her house had been paid. That wasn't likely. She and Wally now had an opportunity to get ahead a little.

"Is Sara here?" she asked. "I need to talk to her for just a minute, if you don't mind."

"I wasn't aware you knew Sara."

"She's a member of the Hook and Needle Club."

He grinned. "Ah, yes. I remember now. Peggy thought it would be good for Sara to become involved in something other than working in the kitchen here. And she was right. Everyone needs something beyond work." He made a face. "I'm one to talk." He spread his hands over the papers in front of him. "I really need to make the transition com-pletely to computer, but old habits die hard." He put his glasses back on and picked up his pen. "You'll find Sara in the kitchen. Feel free to go on in."

"Thanks, Jeff," Annie said as she got up. "I'll see you later."

She pushed through the swinging doors separating the kitchen from the dining room and entered a room filled with noise from two huge, steaming dishwashers. The damp heat that met her mingled with odors of meat, deep-fryer oil, and hot bleach water from the dish-washing area.

Annie glanced around. The kitchen help wore large white aprons, latex gloves, and hairnets. One fellow chopped an entire bunch of celery into perfect bite-size pieces in about ten seconds with a few deft motions of his knife. A woman peeled a pile of potatoes, and it seemed her hands almost moved quicker than the eye could detect. Annie knew most restaurants used boxed food, dried potato flakes, prepackaged salads, and canned vegetables, but The Cup & Saucer cooks made their meals as fresh as the seasons could provide. That's why it was one of the most popular places to eat in town.

Standing at the bank of stainless steel industrial-size sinks, Sara scoured a large, deep pot, her face, flushed pink with the effort of cleaning, was a study in concentration. Annie approached her, but the noise of the dishwashers and running water muffled the sound of her steps.

"Hello, Sara," she said.

Sara looked up, startled, and dropped the pot. It crashed to the floor, drawing the attention of everyone in the kitchen. Sara's hazel eyes bulged for a moment, and then she looked around as if seeking a place to run.

"It's OK," Annie said, as she reached down and picked up the pot. "I'm sorry I startled you!"

Sara wordlessly took the pot from Annie and gulped.

"I ... you ..." She put the fingers of one hand to her mouth. "Employees only back here, Annie. I'm sorry."

Annie grabbed the pot before it slipped from the woman's grip again.

"It's all right," she said. "Jeff said I could find you in here, so I'm not trespassing into this space without permission." She smiled and glanced around. "So do you like working here?"

"Kitchen work is about all I know how to do," she replied, somewhat defensively. "Good jobs for someone my age are hard to find. Nobody wants to train an older woman."

"You're not that old, Sara!" Annie said with what she hoped was an encouraging smile. "And besides that, I have good news for you."

"You do?"

Annie nodded. "If you take back this pot and promise not to drop it again," she said, pausing to laugh as she handed it over, "I'll give you something I think you'll appreciate."

Wordlessly, and looking completely mystified, Sara set the pot aside. Annie pulled the list of orders from her purse. She glanced at it, smiling.

"The other day I took those bookmarks you made to The Gift Gallery and to Books Galore in Portland. They loved them! These are orders for more, and both owners want the bookmarks as soon as you can possibly make them."

Sara blinked as if she did not understand.

"I watched you crochet three bookmarks the other day as you sat in the meeting. You're incredibly fast, Sara." When the woman still said nothing, Annie added, "I hope

I didn't step over the line by doing this. But since it's near-ing Christmas, and everyone can use a little extra cash, I just thought ...."

Sara seemed to come to herself then, wiping her damp hands on her apron and finally taking the paper from Annie.

"Oh, my," she said softly, laying the fingers of one hand against her lips as she read the orders.

"I realize it's a big order."

Sara nodded. "And it's so close to Christmas. I mean, will people buy them at this late date?"

Annie laughed softly.

"I think you underestimate the needs of last-minute shoppers. They often forget this person or that, or they need an inexpensive but special gift for someone at the office. Your handmade bookmarks will be a perfect item to sell, especially in bookstores and gift shops."

"Oh, my!" she said again, her eyes swimming. "When you came in, I thought ... well, never mind that." She waved her hand dismissively and blinked back tears. "Thank you, Annie. I'll get started on these tonight." She frowned. "Oh!" This was said with all the buoyancy of air leaving a balloon.

"What is it, Sara?"

"Well, I can make them quickly, and I can make them very pretty. But I don't have a car. How am I going to get to Portland?"

Annie smiled.

"Why, I'll take you, of course."

The woman's eyes, soft and bright, shone in the harsh fluorescent light of the kitchen.

"You've been nicer to me than anyone in my whole life.

Well, except for Peggy, of course. I never thought I'd ever have such good friends again, but you've changed my mind." She looked down and frowned a little. "Not many people have been kind to me unless they want something." She flung back her head and met Annie's eyes, as though questioning what payment Annie might expect from her.

"I don't want anything from you, Sara, except your friendship."

The other workers were watching them, and Annie didn't want Sara to be bothered on her account. She glanced at her watch.

"Alice's furnace went on the blink, and she's staying with me for a few days, so I better get home before she starts worrying that I slid off the road. I don't think she trusts my driving on these wintry Maine roads yet, even though the streets and highways are clear as if it were the Fourth of July."

Something washed over Sara's face—something like happiness.

"Alice is staying at your house? Oh, that's nice!"

"Yes, it is. You know, when you're alone, it's fun to have a friend stay a few days with you."

Sara smiled, her face softening so that Annie saw what a lovely girl she must have been before the cares of life had bored into her.

"Why don't you come up to Grey Gables for dinner tonight?" Annie asked. "It would be such fun for the three of us to get to know each other. Bring your crocheting along, and we'll—"

"Oh, no! I can't do that!" Sara said with such alarm that

Annie took a step back. "I have to work until closing. If I were to leave early, I'd lose this job, and I just can't lose this job."

Annie understood the woman's concern. She gently laid one hand on Sara's forearm and said, "Then we'll just get together when you aren't working. When's your next day off?"

"He hasn't posted our schedules yet," Sara said, scouring the pot she had dropped when Annie spoke to her, as if to prove to anyone watching that she was a good worker. Annie did not want to cause her more worry.

"All right then. If you'll call me, we'll set up a dinner or luncheon, or even breakfast if you prefer. You can let me know at the next Hook and Needle Club meeting."

Sara gave her an odd look and then nodded. Annie hurried back into the dining room so the others would quit looking at them, and Sara could relax. One thing that the nervous, frail-looking woman did not need was more worry on her plate.

Annie returned to Grey Gables and told Alice everything she'd purchased and how she'd asked Aaron Webster to see to it that Sara got her gifts while keeping the givers' identities a secret.

"That poor woman is scared to death she's going to lose her job," Annie said, "though I don't think she has a thing to worry about. She's a hard worker and is good at what she does."

"Good!" Alice said. "You know, Annie, it seems we've taken Sara under our wings."

"I think she needs some people to care about her, don't you?"

"Yes," Alice admitted. "I think she's had some hard knocks."

"Undoubtedly."

"You know," Alice continued, "sometimes people bring hard knocks to their doors—poor choices and all that."

"And sometimes, no matter how hard a person tries, hard knocks follow them," Annie said. "In Sara's case, maybe it's a combination of the two, but I believe she's trying hard to improve her life."

"I hope you're right and that your faith in her isn't misplaced. In any case, I think she's going to love having some new clothes."

"I hope so," Annie said. For Sara Downs, Stony Point's Santa was Alice MacFarlane and Annie Dawson.

— 16 —

The next morning, Alice rang up the furnace repair people. After she hung up the phone, she sat down at the kitchen table and said, "It's going to be a while before my furnace is fixed. The thing is so ancient, they're having trouble finding replacement parts."

"That's too bad," Annie said as she made fresh hot cocoa for the three of them. Noelle sat in her booster seat and enthusiastically colored in an old coloring book Annie had found in a box of toys in the attic. "But I hope you realize I'm more than happy to have you stay right here at Grey Gables as long as you need to. Winters can get so cold and gray and long, even if you have a good friend next door."

Alice nodded, half-listening. "You know," she mused aloud, "if I owned the carriage house, I'd replace that furnace. Then I think I might do some other fixing up too." She sighed, shaking off her thoughts of renovations. "Maybe someday I'll see about buying the place."

"I think that's a fine idea." Annie said, glancing out the window. "The weather forecast says we have a nor'easter blowing in tonight and plenty of snow is expected—again."

Annie cooled Noelle's hot chocolate by adding a bit more milk. She poured it in a bright red sippy cup and gave it to the little girl. "It's very warm—drink it slowly," she cautioned.

Noelle took a drink, smacked her lips, and smiled.

"I don't believe I've ever seen a child get more delight out of simple things than Noelle does," Annie said. "John and Joanna have a lot of fun, but sometimes they're picky about what they eat or wear or play with. Last night, Noelle played with that cardboard box and my old stuffed elephant for an hour or more."

They watched the girl finish her cocoa and then return with renewed zest to the coloring book.

"You're going to miss her when she's gone," Alice said.

Annie nodded and made no response. For the moment, she chose to not even think about the day when Noelle would leave her.

While Alice cleaned up the kitchen, Annie gave Noelle a bath and dressed her in one of the new outfits—tiny maroon corduroy pants that still had to have the hems rolled a couple of turns and the waistband pinned more tightly. A fluffy, sunny yellow sweater with embroidered kittens frolicking on the front was a smidgen too large, but it fit well enough. Thick white socks and sneakers completed Noelle's new ensemble. Annie brushed her fine, blond hair and clipped both sides with yellow barrettes. When Annie was finished with her, Noelle stared at herself in the mirror for a long sober moment, and then she turned and hid her face against Annie's legs.

"Honey, what's wrong? See how pretty you are?"

Noelle buried her face more firmly into Annie's slacks and gripped with tiny fingers. Annie picked her up and was surprised to see how pink the girl's face was. Noelle stole another look at herself and her blush deepened. She looked away.

Did her own reflection embarrass the girl? Perhaps she failed to recognize herself and thought she faced a stranger. Annie had never seen this kind of reaction from a child before. She picked up Noelle and approached the mirror more closely.

"Sweetheart, look in the mirror. That's you. See how pretty you are?"

Keeping her head down, Noelle slid a sideways glance at her reflection. Annie waved at her. Noelle's eyes went from her reflection to Annie's and back to her own. She lifted her head a bit and then raised one hand, sliding her thumb into her mouth as she watched the girl in the mirror doing the same thing. She straightened even more, looking at herself more closely. Annie waved once more. This time, she wriggled her fingers in a tentative wave.

Annie held her closer to the mirror, and then tapped her fingernails on it. She waved again.

"Hi, Noelle!" she said brightly at the reflection. "Look how nice you look with your pretty yellow sweater and new pants." She plucked at the items while she spoke. Noelle looked down at her clothes and then looked in the mirror at them. Her gaze went to her hair, and she touched the barrettes.

"You're very pretty," Annie told her.

"Pretty!" she said around the thumb.

"Yes. Even with that thumb in your mouth. I know what we should do! Let's take your picture! OK?"

Noelle grinned.

Annie carried her downstairs and fetched her camera from the small desk drawer in the living room.

"Let's put you right here in front of the fireplace," Annie said, "and you may hold your bear."

She settled the child near the hearth with the cheery fire throwing its warm glow across Noelle's fine features and hair. She took several shots and even a few in which she was able to persuade the girl to take her thumb from her mouth. Annie knew one day these pictures would be bittersweet, but for that moment they were very sweet indeed. Noelle went looking for the bear's companion, the elephant Binky-Boo.

A few minutes later, Alice came out of the kitchen and into the living room. Noelle ran to her from the library where she'd been playing. She had Binky-Boo in one hand and her new, nameless bear in the other.

"Hi!" she said, twirling with both arms straight out. "I pretty!"

Alice dramatically lifted both hands, opened her eyes wide, and gasped aloud, "My goodness, Madame Noelle! Look at you. You're gorgeous!"

Noelle twirled some more until she staggered and fell to the floor, laughing. A moment later, she got to her feet a bit unsteadily, but hollered, "Look! Look!" and went running back to the library. When she returned a few seconds later, she had neither elephant nor bear, but clutched a large plush, snow white teddy bear.

"That's nearly half your size!" Alice said, laughing. She looked at Annie. "That was in the gifts from Stony Point's Santa, wasn't it?"

"It was. That and a couple of other toys which I decided to save for Christmas." She glanced out the window. "I've been listening to the radio, and that storm's coming fast. I'm going to go check on the old man before it gets here. I've packed him some food, just in case he needs or wants it." She glanced at Alice. "You don't mind watching Noelle, do you?"

"Of course not. But if you're going to check on him, please hurry and get back. We don't want you to get caught on the beach in a nor'easter."

"I don't want that, either. I'll make it quick."

She layered on her heavy winter outerwear and then picked up the basket of food.

"I'll have a good hot lunch ready for you when you return," Alice said.

Annie gave her a big smile. "Thank you, dear friend. I'm sure that will be most welcomed!"

True to her promise, Annie walked as swiftly as possible, blinking against the wind and cold, a very real feeling of déjà vu tagging her heels like a familiar old dog. She was carrying more food even though she was now pretty sure the old man could afford whatever he needed. Something was driving her back to the old shack—a deep-rooted feeling that he needed her, even if he didn't need the food.

As she approached the shack, it gave the appearance of complete desertion. She paused and stared hard. Had he finally come to his senses and left this desolate place? Or was the aura of abandonment simply a product of her hopeful imagination? She hurried along, the basket on her arm growing heavier with each step.

She knocked on the weathered and damp-swollen door, waiting only a few moments before she knocked again.

There was a noise inside, a voice, perhaps, or a cough and then the sound of something moving.

"Hello!" she called. "It's Annie Dawson from Grey Gables."

She heard a fumbling at the door, possibly the scrape of a key turning a lock. The door opened, but she saw no one.

"Come in, come in," said an irritable, weak voice. "Shut the door and be quick about it."

Hurriedly, she stepped inside and closed the door. Inside, the shack was surprisingly warm, but she suspected it felt that way because the last several minutes she'd been in bitter cold. The fragrance of smoke, bacon, and coffee predominated the scent of old wood and the sea. She blinked to adjust her eyes to light that seeped through foggy, dirt-encrusted windows.

The old man sat across the small room from her, his ancient chair near the old wood-burning stove. A dappled blue enamel pot of coffee simmered. Annie ignored everything around her as she focused on his drawn face.

"You don't look so good," she said.

"Thank you." He scowled and refused to meet her eyes.

"In fact, I think you look quite ill." When he said nothing, she approached and placed her hand on his forehead. "I believe you may be running a tiny bit of a temperature."

He shrugged. "Highly unlikely. I'm just sitting too close to this stove." Finally, he lifted his eyes and met her gaze.

"So ... you want to look at my tongue or in my ears? That's what doctors do, isn't it, even if you have a stubbed toe or a sore thumb. Here, look at my eyes and tell me if I'm going to live."

He sat forward, pulled down his lower lids for a moment, then dropped his hands to his lap and sat back.

"Is your throat sore?" she asked. "Do you have a headache?"

He glared at her, and then said, "No. It's my arthritis."

"Arthritis. And you've been outside, dealing with this weather, living in this place that has cracks in the wall big enough to throw a cat through it." She pointed to a rather large crack just opposite her. A draft strong enough to stir a paper on top of the table whistled through it. "Have you at least been eating?"

"Lady, I have eaten quite well since you took me into your tribe." He frowned. "I wish you'd sit down. You make me twitchy, standing there that way."

She glanced around. The only place to sit was on the edge of his very narrow bed. She settled there.

"Do you take medication for your arthritis?"

He now leaned back in his chair again, eyes closed and face registering pain.

"I do."

"Have you taken any today?"

He did not reply, and she repeated the question. He opened one eye, stared at her for a time, and then heaved a deep sigh.

"I would if I could get the bottle open."

She glanced around, taking notice of certain details in the room to be addressed later. "Where's the bottle? I can open it for you."

"Maybe. You, a small army and a blowtorch. It's over there on the shelf by the sink." He dipped his head toward the other side of the tiny room.

Annie found it and hefted it in her palm. "This feels full."

"It's a new bottle."

She eyed the prescription label. "And is your name Graham Cartwright?"

His lips thinned as if he were annoyed. "Yes."

She studied him for a minute, her eyes narrowed in thought. "Why do I know that name?"

"You just read it; that's how you know it. Now open the bottle."

Annie realized the more secrets she uncovered, the angrier he grew. At this point, she didn't care if he got mad. She read the date on the label.

"You've had this script for three days! And you've not been able to open it at all?"

He shook his head. "I didn't realize until I got home that they'd given me a childproof cap." He held up hands that looked knobby and painful. "A two-year old could open that bottle before I could. If I hadn't hurt so much, I would've taken it right back to them."

"I'll take care of it for you on one condition."

He narrowed his eyes.

"I've never liked for a woman to say that to me. The 'one condition' usually means something worse than the current situation."

"In this case, you may very well think so, but here it is. I want you to gather some of your things and come with me to Grey Gables."

He started to sit up stiffly but then winced and remained unmoving.

"I will not."

"I'll help you. All you'll need is your clothes and your medicine." She glanced around. "This pile of toys and electronics, along with all that wrapping paper, it will be all right here in your house until the storm is over." She gave him a sharp no-nonsense look. "It's a big storm, and it's coming fast. I don't want to get caught in it."

"Then leave right now."

She went on as if she had not heard him, "And I don't want you getting caught in it either. We haven't a lot of time. I'm sure you can't move too fast, so let's get your things together."

He stayed where he was. Frustration edged closer to anger as she stared at him.

"Come on, *please*," she said. "I can't leave you—in your condition—in this awful little shack with a nor'easter blowing in. You'll freeze to death here." He blinked mildly at her, and it seemed he wouldn't budge, ever. Annie pulled out the best argument she could think of.

"Who will get all those gifts if Stony Point's Santa freezes to death?"

～ 17 ～

*H*e glowered at her. In fact, if his gaze had burned any hotter, the air around him might have burst into flames.

"So you saw me the other night," he said flatly. "And now you know my secret." His jaw tightened briefly, and then he went on. "A woman like you will spread the news faster than an Australian bushfire. If I go with you, I'll have to deal with the media and all your nosy neighbors."

Annie glowered back at him.

"What do you mean, a woman like me? You don't know me."

He waved one hand.

"I know your kind. Do-gooders and caretakers. Mother hens to the world, looking for people to hover over and smother with attention." He pointed a finger at her. "You're just the type to run around telling every piece of gossip you can dig up, but you cache it in terms of 'I'm just trying to help.'"

Anger fueled by this unwarranted attack ran white-hot through Annie. She got up and paced a few steps. She closed her eyes, took a deep breath or two, and silently counted to ten—and then to twenty.

She looked at him, swallowing her anger as best she could. He met her eyes squarely. But rather than the flinty gaze she expected to see pinned on her, she read something else in his eyes: deep pain and loneliness, barely concealed by his crotchety defense.

With a start, Annie realized this old man yearned for her friendship. He longed for care, comfort, and companionship. Obviously those feelings frightened him, and the only way he felt safe was to strike out, pretending he didn't care. At that moment in his life, the old man before her needed someone, probably more than he ever had before. Annie said a silent prayer of thanks that she had kept her anger in check.

"I'm not falling for that," she said softly with a small smile. "Get your things and let's be on our way."

His lips curled in a snarl, and he waved one hand in a gesture of dismissal. "Pfft!"

She glanced around, saw a suitcase under the narrow bed and pulled it out. An older suitcase, without wheels, it was made of fine leather that was stitched meticulously and obviously very expensive. She opened it and saw it contained underwear, socks, pajamas and a robe. She added a stack of clothes piled on the small table. A book Graham Cartwright had been reading was laid facedown near him. He grabbed for it as she picked it up, but she stepped back and wagged a finger at him.

"If you want to read more of this suspense novel, you have to come with me," she told him as she tucked it in with his clothes and closed the suitcase. "I've read it, and I have to say, the best part is the last third of the book. It looked like you're only about halfway through it." She gave him a beatific smile and snapped shut the two clasps.

He glowered, but she was pretty sure she saw a smile lurking behind the scowl.

"You're a wily one, all right," he said.

She put the suitcase beside the door. Then she opened the thermos she'd brought and poured him a cup of coffee.

"This is still hot, so drink up. 'Warm up your innards,' as my neighbors in Texas used to say."

"Texas," he sneered, but he took the cup with both hands. If by scoffing at her home state he thought he'd engage her in a quarrel, he failed miserably. Annie stood placidly while he drank the coffee. As soon as he drained the cup, she took it from him, rinsed it, and put in on the small towel next to the sink. Then she examined the heavy wool sweater he wore.

"That'll do." She eyed his trousers. "You have longjohns on under there?"

"I fail to see that my underwear is any of your business."

"Under normal circumstances, it isn't. But today is exceptional." When he did not respond, she added, "If you won't tell me, I'll look for myself!" She reached for the hem of his trousers, and he pulled his leg back.

"Young woman, you are out of control. Keep your hands to yourself. And yes, I'm wearing thermal underwear and heavy socks. Does that satisfy you?"

Annie smiled. "Yes, thank you. Now put your wraps on, because it's going to be a freezing walk to my house, so I want you as warmly bundled as possible."

"Harrumph!" Cartwright exclaimed.

Annie took the mackinaw off the hook and held it near the stove to warm it.

"Please put on your hat, scarf, and gloves," she said as if he were her young grandson and not a man who was at least twenty-five years her senior. "By the time you do that, this coat will be warm as toast."

He continued to glower. When he didn't move, she put the coat on the bed, settled a faux fur-lined winter hat on his head and pulled down the earflaps.

"Tie that and then wrap this muffler around your neck … all the way up to your chin and leave it a little loose so you can pull it over your face."

"Will you quit hounding me?"

"I will if you'll put your wraps on. Oh, and before I forget, do you take one pill or two?" She opened the medicine bottle.

"One," he said, fussing with the hat.

"Don't you dare take that hat off!" scolded Annie. She shook a single tablet into her palm, allowing him to see it before putting it back in the bottle. "Now, when you have your hat tied, your muffler wrapped, and your coat on and buttoned up, I'll give you your tablet, but not until then."

She hated bribing him with the medicine, especially as he needed it so much. She knew, however, that if she gave it to him right then, he'd stay in his chair, refusing to leave the shack. That would mean he'd remain in a place where he could eventually freeze to death.

Pinning a steady glare on her as she once more held his coat near the stove, he stood up and wrapped the long muffler several times around his neck, leaving some loose for his face just as she had instructed.

"Good!" she said, helping him put on his coat. "But you forgot to tie the hat. And button your coat, all the way up."

He turned from her as he grasped the ties to the hat.

"I'll put away this food. Nothing in here will ruin if it gets frozen."

She added the canned soups to the shelf where he had a can of corn and one of beans. The bread went into a plastic container where only two slices remained. The butter would be fine in its plastic tub. A quick survey told her the rest of his rations were low.

"What would you have done for food if I hadn't shown up today?" she asked, turning to him. He still had his back to her. She thought about how stubborn he was, and then she realized something about his rounded shoulders and bent head that seemed odd.

"Mr. Cartwright?" she said, touching his shoulder. He did not jerk away as she expected. Beneath her palm, she felt his shoulder quiver. Concerned, she went around to his front and saw his fingers unmoving on the buttons of his unfastened coat. She noted the ties for his cap hung loose and open. "Having trouble?" she asked softly.

"No," he growled and began fumbling with the buttons, but his fingers seemed like impediments rather than tools. "Go away! You've caused enough ...." Then his voice cracked. He took a heaving breath, and to Annie's shock, he began to sob. "I can't ... I can't ..." He shook his hands as if trying to fling them away. "They don't work anymore!"

Annie yearned to comfort him. She longed to wrap her arms around his neck and pull him closer, to let him weep out his anger and frustration, but she had a feeling he'd hate that. She did not want to make him feel pathetic or pitiable. Stony Point's Santa wanted steel and determination;

she could give him that. She poured his water, gave him his medicine, and watched him gulp it gratefully. Guilt rose in her like bile—hot and bitter—but she had done what she felt was right to save him from himself. And she wasn't finished.

"Here. Let me get this hat tied tightly. There! Does that feel snug enough? Not too tight?"

He nodded silently. She quickly buttoned the mackinaw and then pulled the collar up and adjusted the muffler. She paused, her hands resting on his shoulders, and looked into his tear-filled eyes. She read humiliation in their depths, knowing his embarrassment of being virtually helpless to his disease.

"Listen," she said with all the gentleness nature had given her, "don't let this condition get to you. Everyone has limitations, and right now, yours is aching, stiff, painful joints. The great thing about having friends ...," she said, pausing to make sure he understood what she was saying. "The great thing about *true* friends is that we help each other. In return, we accept help when it's offered. No fuss, no muss. We just do it." She tapped her palms against both his shoulders twice for emphasis, and then dropped her hands and smiled. "Now, let's get these gloves on you, and let's get going before the storm decides to be our companion."

She helped him with his gloves, tugged on her own and opened the door.

"I think we may be a little too late," he said.

She looked outside. Snow had started, thick and fast, seeming to fall sideways as wind howled in from the northeast.

He shut the door.

"We're staying right here," he said. "You brought food,

and when my hands work again, I'll bring in some wood. We'll be all right."

Annie stared at the old wooden door that kept out the howling storm. She'd brought some food, but not a lot. Now that she had been in the shack for a while, she realized even with a fire in the old stove, it was cold in there. The pile of wood she'd seen near the door was pitifully small. Her thoughts turned to Grey Gables, to Alice and Noelle. If Annie did not return soon, Alice would be worried sick. And Noelle ... she simply could not allow Noelle to feel abandoned again. A few hours at most were all she would ever leave that child.

"We have to go," she said. "Too much depends on us."

"No! I can't walk in that cold wind. I won't be able to move in the morning."

"Listen to me," she said, turning deaf ear to his needs for the moment. "For the sake of a loving friend and a sweet but damaged little girl, you have to forget about yourself and trust me in this. We have to go."

"Then you go. I'm staying."

"No, you aren't." She grabbed his arm as he made a move away from the door. "If you don't come with me to Grey Gables, I'll call the police when I get there to come and get you for your own safety. In fact, now that I think about it, that may be best the thing to do, anyway."

"No!" he snapped, snarling at her like a rabid wolf. "I won't be taken from my own home by the police. Do you think I'm some kind of criminal?"

"No, I do not. But I think you don't care about your own safety."

He glowered and fumed wordlessly; then at last he gave in.

"If we must, we must. You have my medicine?"

"It's in my coat." She patted her deep pocket. "Right here."

"I have a feeling I'm going to need it more than ever after this."

"Yes, you probably will. But Grey Gables is warm and comfortable. You can have a hot bath, and a nice bed in which to recover, and the best food in Maine."

She smiled at him and was rewarded with a scowl, but beneath it laid naked gratitude.

"Let's go," he said, taking her arm.

She opened the door, and they stepped into the storm.

~ 18 ~

The walk out of the cove seemed to take forever. Graham Cartwright's steps were slow and laborious, but Annie was determined to get him to Grey Gables, even if she had to carry the old man across her shoulder like a sack of potatoes. The icy wind heaved an assault with an almost-human ferocity, and the suitcase she carried seemed to add weight as the duo pushed forward through the frigid gale.

Annie glanced at him. His face was a mask of controlled torture—his jaw set and his eyes watery. She stopped, put down the case and said, "You need to have this muffler pulled up to cover the lower half of your face."

She expected him to argue, to shove her hand away. Instead he waited stoically as she adjusted the long crocheted scarf around his lean jawline, mouth, and nose.

"Those stitches are heavy enough to keep out the wind, but loose enough to let in air, so you'll be able to breathe."

He nodded, and they walked on. At one point, he stumbled over a piece of driftwood and grabbed Annie's hand. She allowed him to cling to the safety of her arm, hoping she did not trip or fall as they walked.

Once they struggled out of the mouth of the cove and onto the wind-whipped stretch of beach that would lead them to Annie's home, the wind became an ally rather than enemy. It drove them forward, hustling the pair as if rushing them to shelter.

"I can't …," he gasped loudly above the sound of the wind, "walk this fast."

"But if we don't, the wind will knock us down." Annie gave him an encouraging smile, even though it seemed her icy face might split from the effort. "Just hang onto me, and you'll be all right. Look. Grey Gables is just ahead."

At the sight of her home's familiar roofline, Annie felt like weeping for joy. The man followed her gaze and nodded.

"Too far to go back now," he said.

"Yes! We can't stop. Just a little farther."

Soon they reached the winding path that led up from the shoreline to Annie's yard. That path presented a challenge, and the old man stared at it in dismay. On a good day, anyone could walk the path easily, but not today. The wind was again their foe as it now slammed them sideways, scratching at their eyes like an angry cat. Annie feared for Graham's safety.

"Listen, Mr. Cartwright. Here's what I'm going to do. I'm leaving your suitcase here. It'll be all right until I come back for it, but I need both hands free to help us get up this path." She sat it down nearby, and then she put her right arm around his waist, grasped his left hand with her own and said, "Let's take it easy going up."

"I can't go on," he said. "This cold has worked into my joints like a frozen blade. How can I climb up a snowy trail?"

"Look at me." She gently turned his face away from the hurdle that loomed before him. "We're going to do it one step at a time. Don't look at how far we have to go.

Hang onto me. Put your trust in God and keep your hand in mine." She paused. There was fear in his eyes, but she read determination there too. "All right. Ready?" He nodded. "Remember, one step at a time."

His hand gripped her, crushing it painfully even through the layers of their heavy gloves. With Annie testing for ice on their ascent with the toe of her boot, the pair made their way up. At the top, he leaned against her, gray-faced and breathless. His appearance alarmed her, but shelter and warmth were near, and she could not allow him to fade this close to safety.

"Just a little farther," she encouraged.

"I can't make it up those steps to that porch," he gasped. "I can't!"

"We won't have to." She guided him to the back of the house where the only step was the one that went from the flagstone patio to the kitchen door. Carefully they walked across the icy rocks, and she helped him up the step and through the door.

Inside the kitchen with its sunny yellow walls, the warmth welcomed Annie and Graham like a mother's embrace. A pot of clam chowder simmered with tiny bubbling sighs. The aroma of baking bread seemed like the very breath of life.

She looked at him, his milky eyes and stark-white forehead alarmed her. Without letting go, she led him to the chair closest to the warm stove and settled him there. She yanked off her gloves and pitched them on the table and then pulled the muffler free of his mouth and nose, and unbuttoned the top button of his mackinaw.

"Alice," she called, trying not to let panic strain through her voice. "Here, Mr. Cartwright, let me take off this cap and muffler." She looked toward the kitchen door. "Alice!"

A moment later she heard footsteps running down the staircase. Annie was unwinding the muffler when Alice practically skidded into the kitchen.

"Annie, for goodness' sake!" she cried. "I was worried sick! I just put Noelle down for her nap, and you—" She broke off abruptly, her eyes widening as she saw Annie's companion.

"Would you please fix some hot tea?" When Alice seemed glued to the spot, Annie said, rather sharply, "*Alice!*"

Alice blinked and looked at her.

"Yes. Hot tea. Yes, of course. The water in the kettle is probably still warm, I'll just bring it to a boil."

She met Annie's eyes and signaled a thousand questions in her gaze, but Annie turned back to the man.

"Do you want to leave your coat on?"

He nodded.

Annie knelt by his chair and removed the glove from his right hand. His fingers were icy. She chaffed them gently until she felt them loosen, and then she did the same with his left hand.

Alice poured scalding water over a tea bag in a large white mug.

"Sugar?" Alice asked.

The old man nodded.

"Cream?"

His brows dipped, and he shook his head slightly.

Alice added a spoonful of sugar in the tea, paused, and

then added a little more. "I think you could use a bit more," she said. "Here you go."

Annie reached for it, but he growled at her and allowed Alice to settle the warm mug in his hands.

"Don't burn yourself," Alice cautioned.

"I'm not a child," he croaked, lifting the mug to his lips.

Both women watched as he drank the entire cup of tea without lowering it, sipping carefully at first and finally draining it. He met Annie's gaze over the mug's rim before setting it on the table. His eyes had lost that alarming opaque cast.

"You look better," she said.

"Harrumph!" he snorted. "Dragging me miles through a blizzard and along a frozen beach, bullying me to keep going when I wanted to stop and rest. I'm eighty-five years old. I have a right to look bad!"

Annie saw through the bluster immediately.

"And if I had not 'bullied' you, we'd still be out there in the cold wind and snow. And we did not come miles."

"It felt like miles, even leagues. I may never be able to move again."

Alice poured him another cup of tea and put the sugar bowl near his hand. He sweetened it, drank it, and she filled the cup a third time. By the time he had finished the third cup, color had returned to his face. He breathed normally and no longer looked stunned with cold. He turned his gaze to Alice, surveying her quite leisurely.

"And who are you, Server of Tea?" he said at last. To Annie, he sounded remarkably stronger than he had at any point that day. Could it be that what she feared would

debilitate him had not been the trauma she'd thought it
could be? Perhaps the old man, used to hardship and frugal
living, had more strength than she realized.

"Alice MacFarlane," she said. "I'm Annie's next-door
neighbor." She put out her left hand. "And your name is ...?"

"My hands hurt far too much right now to do the 'Hail
fellow, well met!' business. My name is Graham Cartwright."
Alice's jaw dropped. He smiled slightly. "Ha! I see by that
shocked look on your face that my name is familiar to you.
Not so with your altruistic friend here." He shifted his gray
eyes to Annie. "She hasn't the slightest clue who I am."

"I said your name was familiar to me, but right now,
it doesn't matter who you are. I'm concerned about your
health," she said. "You seem to have recovered your sharp
tongue quite adequately. Let's see if you can move other
parts of your body. How about if we take off your wraps?"

He looked her up and down.

"If *we* are going to take off wraps, you go first," he said.

She quickly removed her hat and scarf. She retrieved
Graham's medicine from her coat pocket and placed it on
the table before taking off her coat. She then handed it to
Alice who hung it on a rack near the back door. Alice stood
silently as she watched the unfolding scene.

"Now you," Annie told him.

He held her gaze for a long moment before reaching up
and fumbling with the ties of his cap. His jaw clenched with
the effort, and pain flared in his eyes. Annie ached to help
him, but she knew he needed to prove to her and—more
importantly—to himself that he was still strong and capable
of taking care of his own needs.

At last the stiff fingers worked the ties loose, and he yanked off the cap. It took a while, but eventually he unfastened all the coat buttons. He stood, slowly and painfully, and tugged his arms free of the coat. Alice took it from him. He glowered at Annie as he unwound the muffler as if its very length was a plot against him.

"Did it!" he chortled weakly, fixing a steely gaze on Annie. "Happy?"

"Immensely!" She grinned impishly at him as Alice hung up his winter wear. She turned to Alice. "That food smells fabulous. Is it nearly ready?"

As if on cue, the timer on Gram's beloved old range pinged.

"Yes," Alice said, smiling. "Mr. Cartwright, the powder room is just down the hall on the left if you'd like to freshen up. When you're ready, I'll have you a nice bowl of clam chowder and some freshly baked bread ready."

To Annie's utter shock, the old man's eyes twinkled at her friend.

"I look forward to that with much anticipation, my dear."

The two women watched him make a slow and careful exit from the kitchen. As soon as the bathroom door closed, Alice turned to her, eyes wide and whisper-squealed.

"Annie! Did he mean that? Do you really not know who he *is*?"

Annie spread her hands in a helpless gesture. From the bathroom came the sound of water rushing from the faucet.

"His name seems familiar, but I'm not making the connection at all."

"Oh, for goodness' sake!" Alice said, rolling her eyes. "Excuse me a moment."

She hurried out of the kitchen and a few moments later returned with several books from the library. The sound of running water in the bathroom continued. Annie figured Mr. Cartwright was comforting his aching hands in the water's flow.

"Graham Cartwright," Alice said, plunking down the stack on the table and laying her hand on the top one, "and these are just three from your grandfather's collection in the library."

Annie eyed the books in surprise as Alice handed her one. *Tracks of the Spy*, a thick volume with the Soviet Union's hammer and sickle menacingly displayed on its red-and-black cover.

"I remember who he is now!" Annie said, in awe of the books before her, each one with Graham Cartwright's name on its spine. "I remember seeing Grandpa in his leather chair, smoking his pipe, totally lost in Mr. Cartwright's spy novels."

"I think Charlie had every one that had been published up to the time of his death. Your grandpa was never one to do anything halfway." The two gawped at the books; then Alice added, "Just think, Annie. Wouldn't your grandfather be thrilled to know his favorite author was in his house right now?"

The water in the bathroom finally shut off, and the door opened. Slow steps approached the kitchen, and Graham Cartwright stepped inside, watching his fingers flex and relax.

"That warm water eased my—" He broke off as he looked up and saw the books.

"What's this?" he murmured and approached the table. He took a book from the stack. "Hmm. *The Spy at Dawn*. I wrote much of this one while recovering from surgery. A lot of pain involved in that book." He gave a dry chuckle, and then shot a look at Alice. "I take it you are alleviating your friend's ignorance of her refugee's identity?"

"Mr. Cartwright, my focus was not on who you were or what you've done, but on getting you to a safe place where you would be comfortable, warm, and well-fed." She paused to let this sink in. When he said nothing, she continued, "I hope you're starting to feel better, and I apologize for putting you through the ordeal of walking in such fierce weather. But you're here now, and if you'll sit, we'll give you a good, hot meal."

"Ever the clucking mother hen, aren't you?" he said grudgingly, but settled himself at the table with his books nearby.

While Alice cut thick slices of her hot, homemade bread, Annie dished up a generous bowlful of chowder for him. She poured a tall glass of milk for him, and then she put more water in the teakettle and put it on the stove to heat.

"There you go, Mr. Cartwright," Alice said as she placed the bread before him on the table. She patted his shoulder. "Eat up. There's plenty more."

He smiled at her in a way that Annie thought curious, as if he had an instant, fatherly affection for her friend.

"Thank you, my dear. I hope you'll join me." He shifted a bit on his chair and pinned a gaze on Annie as he shook out a napkin and laid it in his lap. "You and my *rescuer,* of course."

"Now you be nice to Annie," Alice said, smiling, almost flirting, as she sat down. "She's a dear. I think you needed to be rescued, all alone in some old shack. Look how thin you are!"

"Perhaps you're right," he said, picking up his spoon. He

glanced at Annie. "I suppose I do owe you my gratitude, mad-
am. I surely might have perished without your intervention."

Annie smiled, realizing this was as close to an apology
for his rudeness as she was apt to receive. "I think that is
highly likely," she said.

Alice watched him spoon in the chowder and bite into
the soft, buttery slice of warm bread.

"Ah, manna from heaven," he said, nodding.

"Eat all you want," Alice said eagerly. "You must keep
up your strength so you can write more wonderful books!
Annie's grandfather, Charles Holden, had an entire collection of your books up until his death. I used to borrow—"

"I no longer write," he said brusquely, a dark frown on
his thin face. "In fact, I will never pick up the pen again!"

~ 19 ~

"What?" Alice squawked. "You don't write anything at all? I know it's been a while since I saw a new title from you, but I was hoping maybe that's why you came to Stony Point … to hole up and write a new novel."

Before the man had a chance to respond, tiny steps came running along the hallway, and Noelle charged into the kitchen with her old teddy bear in one arm and her thumb in her mouth.

"Hungry!" she said around the thumb. She ran toward Annie, halting as she caught sight of a stranger in their midst. Annie saw fear leap into the child's eyes and went quickly to pick her up.

"I'm thinking you had a rather short nap," she said to Noelle.

"That she did," Alice said. "But when Noelle smells food, she comes running, even from a deep sleep!"

Graham studied the girl as he chewed; then he pointed with his spoon and said, "I assume that is what someone left here for you to care for?"

Annie did not like the way he spoke as if Noelle were a potted plant someone had asked her to water.

"This is Noelle," she said. "She's very sweet, but very shy."

"And completely without known relatives?"

"At this point, yes."

He stared at Noelle a moment longer before turning back to his chowder.

"I perceive you plan to keep the child."

"Not forever," Annie replied, somewhat hesitantly. "But obviously she needs looking after and to be cared for. When the time comes, well, I'll deal with whatever I have to deal with."

Graham turned to Alice and dipped his head toward Annie. "Mother hen to the world."

Rather than taking the term as an insult, Annie chose to look at it as a compliment.

"Thank you," she said. "I believe that's part of why I'm here, to help others."

"Let's feed this little one," Alice said. Annie kissed Noelle's cheek and settled her into the booster seat. Alice dipped out a small serving of chowder and buttered a half slice of bread.

"You must believe that about yourself as well, don't you, Mr. Cartwright?" Annie said as she placed the food before Noelle.

He looked up.

"What's that?"

"That you are here to help others. I mean, look at all the wonderful things you've done for this town—"

He turned fierce anger on Annie.

"I knew it!" he nearly shouted. "I knew you were the kind of woman who went around sharing every tidbit of knowledge you can possibly dredge up for the rest of the world to devour."

"Nanny!" Noelle cried, and Annie gathered her up protectively.

"Mr. Cartwright, I will not be shouted at in my own home, and you will refrain from outbursts in front of this sensitive little girl. Firstly, as I told you earlier, I am not the kind of woman who goes around gossiping, and secondly, I did not broadcast your identity to the world. Alice lives next door. She's my best friend, and she visits me often."

"Is that so?" he asked Alice.

"Of course." She looked back and forth between the two of them. "Annie told me about meeting you on the beach, and she has been so worried about your well-being and confused why you've been so rude to her. So when she thought she saw you after you left Noelle's gifts on the porch, I refused to believe her. And you can rest assured she has not mentioned your presence to anyone else." She paused. "But now that you're here, and I know who you are and know that you are a gentleman of quality—well, forgive me for asking—are *you* Stony Point's Santa?"

His eyebrows plunged downward in the most frightening scowl Annie had ever seen, and he shoved his chair back from the table with remarkable strength.

"Busybodies and do-gooders!" Graham shouted. "Saving the world while displaying all your good deeds so the entire world can lay accolades at your feet!"

Annie grabbed Noelle, and she whisked the child out of the room.

"Mr. Cartwright!" Alice exclaimed as Annie went down the hall. "What in the world is wrong with you? Annie and I understand your need for anonymity, and we'll keep your secret. I don't understand why you are so surly to someone who has been nothing but kind to you. She does not deserve your contempt. And if you're Stony Point's Santa, doesn't that automatically make you a 'do-gooder'?" She paused briefly. "Frankly, after this little display, I'm not sure I'd buy your next book, even if it was a Pulitzer Prize winner!"

Annie was snuggling Noelle in the living room, but Alice's voice had carried well, as it usually did when she was angry. She stomped into the living room and plopped down on the sofa next to Annie.

"Whatever is the matter with that man?" she said, gesturing in the general direction of the kitchen. "I haven't seen anyone so rude since the last time I visited New York City and tried to get a cab."

"I don't know what his problem is," Annie said, "but I won't have Noelle exposed to angry shouting. She's been through enough in her short life, and Nanny's house should be a safe haven for her."

"I agree," Graham Cartwright said from the doorway of the living room, surprising both women. Noelle snuggled closer in Annie's arms. "I harbor no special affection for children, but I wish them no harm. I certainly would never want to frighten a little girl who has had a hard life. I apologize to you, Mrs. Dawson, for being an old crank. I have lived alone too long. Truly I'm trying to mend my selfish ways." He offered all three of them a smile. "I hope you will accept my apology."

Annie and Alice exchanged looks, and then they turned their eyes to him. Annie had never been one to turn away an apology or bear any grudges.

"Thank you, Mr. Cartwright. I accept your apology. But I must ask that you respect us enough never to shout in my home again, unless it's to shout with joy."

He inclined his head once.

Alice took in a deep breath and blew it out. "I have never liked for anyone to disrespect my friends," she said and paused as her words sunk in, "but I understand you're in pain, and you had a long, treacherous hike to this house. I, too, accept your apology."

He bowed graciously.

"May I humbly request all three of you rejoin me for lunch?"

"Yes. I think that's a good idea," Annie said.

*   *   *   *

The meal resumed, and the brief silence was broken by the sounds of spoons dipping into bowls and Annie murmuring reassurances to Noelle.

"This is probably the finest clam chowder I've ever eaten," Graham said. "Creamy, hearty—absolutely perfect. And the bread is ..." He bunched his fingertips and kissed them. "Delicioso!"

"Thank you," Alice said, smiling.

"Alice is the best cook in Stony Point," Annie said. "Noelle, sweetheart, don't use your fingers to eat chowder." She placed the spoon back in the girl's tiny fist.

Noelle kept eating, but shot suspicious glances at Graham throughout the meal.

"I have brownies," Alice said when they were

finished. "My own special recipe, with chocolate chunks and cashews."

"My goodness," Graham said, his gray eyes alight, "I should have knocked on your door and asked for room and board before this, Mrs. Dawson."

"Please call me Annie. As I said, Alice is the best cook, but she lives next door. If you'd knocked on my door, you'd have had to have put up with some of my cooking. And you will, because I hope you realize you are *not* going back to that awful little shack."

"I realize you think I should not."

"We won't let you," Alice said.

"No, we won't," Annie agreed. "Finding you on short rations, little wood to burn, in pain from arthritis, unable to open your medicine .... No, you certainly will not be going back there."

He silently observed both women. Annie could see the rebellion on his face, but she refused to let an old man die because of his own stubbornness.

* * * *

As evening approached, the raging storm outside Grey Gables began to die down. Annie sneaked out the back door and walked through the fresh snow back to the beach path, carefully wending her way down to where she and Graham Cartwright had left his suitcase. The wind off the coast had kept it swept clear of snow, but a thin coat of ice encased it. Annie cautiously climbed back up the slope, surprising Graham with his suitcase once she had reached the warm confines of Grey Gables again.

All the bedrooms were upstairs, and knowing he was not ready to climb stairs, Annie settled Graham on the comfy old sofa in the family room that night. At some point, if he wanted a hot bath or shower, he'd have to go upstairs since there was nothing on the main floor but the powder room.

He chose to go to bed just as darkness fell, and Annie did not hear him stir all night. However, early the next morning as she was getting dressed, Annie heard the guest shower. For a moment, she wondered if it was Graham, but logic told her it was Alice.

Annie checked on Noelle, and saw the girl in deep sleep, curled beneath the old quilts Gram had made.

In the kitchen a bit later, she made waffles, bacon, and eggs for breakfast, and she laid places for everyone. Graham—freshly showered, shaved and dressed in jeans and flannel shirt—strode into the room. Right behind him trailed Alice in her robe, yawning, with her auburn hair looking as though she'd slept in a wind tunnel.

"Graham!" Annie said. "That was you in the shower upstairs?" She had coffee simmering and his plate warming in the oven, so she set a plateful of food for him.

He nodded. "Took me a while to go up, but a hot shower has done wonders. I've never been one to molly-coddle myself." He sat down at the table. "The lesson here, ladies, is don't sit around waiting for age to incapacitate you. The more active you are, the more you'll be able to do, even if you have aches and pains. Even when you are as old as I am."

"Good to know," Alice said, sinking into her own chair

and yawning again. "My goodness, I'm sleepy today." She glanced around. "Where's our baby girl?"

Annie cocked her head to one side. "I believe I hear her little bare feet pattering down the hall right now."

Noelle entered the kitchen, face rosy and eyes swollen with sleep. She padded straight to Annie and lifted her arms.

"Sweetheart, go put your slippers on. They're right next to your bed." Annie kissed one soft cheek and put her down. Noelle did not pout or whine, and came back in a minute with her feet cozily inside fuzzy bunny slippers.

Annie settled her in the booster seat. Noelle dove into the waffles and bacon like she had not eaten in days. Graham watched her for a while and then chuckled. "My word, that girl has an appetite."

Annie smiled as Noelle drank her cup of milk with gusto. "Yes, she does. It's hard to believe she's so thin. But she's put on weight in these few days since she showed up. And her little cheeks are not nearly as pallid as they were."

They watched Noelle shove in her last bite of bacon, and she looked at everyone's plate for more.

"We can't have you running out," Graham said. "Here, little girl. Have some of mine." He handed her a strip of crispy bacon. She blinked her large pale eyes at him and then looked at the meat. He held it closer, and she finally grabbed it from his hand.

Alice grinned and winked at Annie.

"Oh, I'm not sure she should have so much bacon," Annie began, but Graham waved away her concern.

"Look at her go. She loves it." He smiled. "Don't you, Noelle?"

She munched happily and grinned, showing the half-chewed food in her mouth. He lifted his brows, as though surprised very young children had no table manners.

"Charming little girl," he said, chuckling as he turned back to his own breakfast.

"I'm so glad to see you feeling better today," Annie said. "I really was quite worried."

"I must admit I feel better this morning than I have for several weeks, even before I came to Maine."

"It's the warmth and good food," Annie suggested. "Well, I should say the warmth indoors."

"I daresay you're right. And having a hot shower almost made me feel like a young man again." He wiggled his eyebrows at Annie in a mock leer.

She laughed at him and waggled a finger. "First you despise me and then you flirt with me. You're a wily fellow, Graham Cartwright."

"You'd better be careful," Alice teased. "Annie's sort of spoken for by a certain public servant."

Annie shot Alice a sideways glance. Graham chuckled, but then sobered.

"Once more, I apologize for my harsh words and surly attitude. I've been too much apart from the rest of humanity, answerable to no one but myself. I don't like what I've become, and it's time for me to make a change."

Annie settled her elbows on the table and rested her chin on her hands. "Once more, you are forgiven," she said. "Do you want to tell us what brought about this change? I promise not to spread it around town."

"I won't either," Alice added.

"I know that," Graham said with a shamefaced smile. "You have been nothing but kind to me, Annie. Alice, you are Annie's true and loyal friend. I've not been around many people like the two of you. In fact, most of my life has been spent in solitude, serving my art and serving myself. When one does that, there is no room for love or concern for anyone else."

"You have no wife and family?" Alice asked.

"Never. Just myself. I knew early on I wanted a career as a writer. And not *just* a writer, but a highly successful one. I could pretend to be noble and say I didn't want to burden another person with penury as I established my career, but the truth of the matter is I didn't want someone demanding my time, attention, and resources. A wife and family would be nothing but an encumbrance."

Annie got up and refilled his cup. "Well, you do have a point," she said as she returned to her place across from him, "and I can see where a young man starting out might avoid attachments of that kind. But what about after your career was established? Didn't you want to share your life with anyone?"

"Never considered it," he said, waving one hand dismissively and shaking his head, "except maybe in the shadowy far reaches of my mind. I traveled the world. I had a home in Key West, an apartment in New York, and another in Zurich. My friends—check that—my circle of acquaintances was other writers, but we rarely spent time together. I had too much research to do. Writing about espionage during the Cold War, while the Cold War was going on, had its own set of rules and pitfalls. A marriage or a close friendship—nothing would have lasted under those circumstances, at least not with me at the proverbial wheel."

Annie sighed. "I find that extremely sad."

"I was extraordinarily successful," he reminded her. "I met my goals and achieved my dreams." He fell silent for a moment, his eyes on the kitchen window, seeing something far beyond anything human vision. "I was happy."

"But something happened, didn't it?" Alice said. "Something changed all that for you."

"Yes," he said so quietly Annie almost couldn't hear him. "The Cold War ended, and I was no longer relevant. That's what kept showing up in reviews: 'The work of Graham Cartwright is no longer relevant.'"

"Oh, my," Annie said, faintly. "But that's been years … and you've written nothing since then?"

He heaved out a huge breath. "I've written a few things, tried my hand at something new—"

"Potty!" Noelle announced, wriggling until Annie was afraid she'd fall.

"Excuse us, Mr. Cartwright—" Annie interjected.

"Call me Graham, please."

"All right. Excuse us, Graham. I need to take care of Noelle, but I'll be right back. I want to pick up where we left off."

He met Annie's eyes, and she saw so much sorrow in his gaze that she wanted to weep. Perhaps Alice saw it too, because she said, "I'll take care of Noelle—give her a bath and the whole works."

"Thank you, Alice," Annie said gratefully, smiling at her friend. She knew this time the old man was opening his heart—and that was rare and golden. She did not want it to slip away.

"Let's go into the living room," she said. "Shall I make us a fresh pot of coffee?"

He patted his thin stomach. "No thank you. I've had plenty of food and coffee this morning."

They settled on the comfortable overstuffed furniture in the living room, Graham in the jade green armchair and Annie on the floral sofa.

Graham's sharp eyes took in the room. He seemed to study every point from the fireplace to the to the hardwood floors to the polished rococo table near the large bay window. But his gaze returned again and again to the large framed cross-stitch ocean vista above the fireplace.

"I have rarely seen a piece of fabric art that I like as well as I do that one."

"It's a Betsy Original. My grandmother, Elizabeth Holden, made it a few years before she died. It's the view from my bedroom window upstairs."

"Ah! Well, she was a true artist."

"She was. She is very well known for her hand-stitched art. Hence the 'Betsy Original,'" Annie explained. "She actually founded the New England Stitch Club, and now there are over fifty chapters in the New England area. And she was a wonderful woman—and a wonderful grandmother."

"Impressive. Did you inherit her skill?"

Annie laughed, a little sadly. "No, not really. But she did teach me to crochet, and I do that rather well. That gold-and-white variegated throw behind you, for instance. I made it last spring. And I made that chocolate-brown one on the wing chair beside the fireplace. The muffler you hated so much yesterday was also my handiwork."

"I see. Well, one thing about that muffler, my neck, chin, lips and nose didn't get frostbitten, so you did a good job."

"We have a wonderful craft club here in Stony Point. The Hook—"

"The Hook and Needle Club. Yes, I know all about it."

She blinked in surprise. "You do? How on earth do you know about—"

Graham gave a dismissive wave of one hand. She realized this was a characteristic of his.

"Let's just say I know some things about Stony Point and leave it at that, shall we?"

Annie's natural curiosity stepped up about a dozen notches. "Did you used to live here?"

"This is my first time in your little community."

"Then you have relatives here?"

"No."

"Friends?"

"I have very few friends. If you and the lovely Alice allow me to count you among them, then let me say I have four friends in Stony Point, Maine." The look he gave her held a strong measure of warning and resistance. Annie knew she needed to tread lightly, or they might be back to where they started.

"Then let me ask you this: Why did you choose Stony Pointers to be the recipients of your anonymous gifts?"

"Why not the good people of Stony Point? Is there something in this hamlet that should repel gift-giving?"

"Of course not. But, if you had never been here, have no family here ... did your friends compel you to come and give?"

"I had no friends here until I arrived," Graham said. "And wipe that puzzled frown from your face, Annie Dawson. If you vow to keep my identity a secret—"

"I've already done that," she reminded him.

"Then I will tell you why I chose to become Father Christmas in this neck of the woods."

~ 20 ~

"It really is no big mystery why I decided to turn a new leaf at this time of year," Graham Cartwright said. "I have hated Christmas for most of my adult life. It got in my way—the noise, the celebration, the overabundance of garish decor. I really felt Christmas was just one more annoyance and distraction in my life. I resented it."

"What changed your mind?"

"Well you may ask, Annie! One does not make an abrupt change overnight … usually. However, a few weeks ago, I had a little scare. I think it may have been a heart attack, but I'm not sure."

"A heart attack! And here you've been living in that old shack, barely a modern convenience to help you, fighting the elements as if you're a man of twenty! My goodness, what did your doctor say?"

"Doctors!" he scoffed. "What do they know beyond keeping a diseased body alive longer than it should be? Perhaps I only had indigestion. The point is, Annie …" He paused to give her a sharp look as though daring her to interrupt him. "The point is the pain stopped me, literally, in my tracks. Pressure in my chest, shortness of breath, tingling up and down my arm. I decided if I were going to die, I'd do so with a measure of decorum, in my bed, not sprawled out on the floor."

"Oh, my," Annie said.

"I went to bed, in the middle of the day. I lay there and waited for death. Death did not come, but sleep did." He leaned forward. "And so did a dream."

Annie felt her eyes grow wide. "Oh, my," she whispered again. "Go on."

"I dreamed my entire life, in capsule form, as if I watched it from someplace far away. I saw the poverty of my childhood, the desperation of my father as he tried to hold the family together during the Great Depression. I witnessed my teenage years, working like a dog at any job I could find, on the outside looking in, but recording it all in my mind, writing a mental story of how I would never be destitute as long as I had breath in my body."

Annie's soft heart ached, but she didn't say a word.

"Then I watched as I moved through young adulthood, saving enough money to leave home so I could shut myself from everything dear to my heart, devoting every waking moment to my craft. The world became my classroom. I learned how to turn a phrase or create a scene that would draw a reader between the pages of a novel."

"You accomplished that!" Annie said. "My grandfather sat immersed in your world as he read your books. I could stand beside him and speak, but sometimes he didn't hear a word I said."

Graham nodded.

"I'm both humbled and appalled. I am humbled that your grandfather stepped into my novels with such devotion. I'm appalled I created stories that did for him what creating them did for me: shutting out others."

"Oh, but he didn't—"

He held up one hand, and she fell silent.

"By the time I was twenty-two years old, my first book was on the *New York Times* best-seller list. And every new book thereafter sold more and more. In my dream that night, I watched my arrogant self turn away in disdain from fellow authors wanting support or fellowship, and from young, green writers who needed a little help or a word of encouragement. I shunned my hardworking parents because I couldn't waste time with them. They were old and needy; I had a public to please and a bank account to fill. Women? I rarely gave them a thought. Children? Even less.

"I saw myself alone in my home, squirreled away in my office, tapping on a typewriter, writing about a life that may or may not reflect the real affairs of the world, and—outside of my opulent domicile—humanity breathed, moved, and lived."

He paused long enough to swallow hard, as though trying not to choke.

"Then, Annie, the dream turned dark—as dark as murky water in a dead pond. A stench rose around me, a hideous odor like nothing I'd ever smelled before, something like death and rot, but far worse. From that far place of observation, I looked down into my bedroom and saw myself, or what was left of myself, decayed almost beyond recognition. At that moment, I knew that heart attack had been real. I was dead. But rather than die with grace and decorum as I thought I would do, I had died alone and unnoticed, never missed, while the world outside continued on without me."

Annie bit her lower lip and said nothing.

"I felt myself falling from that far-off observatory, plummeting toward my rotted body. I screamed, clutching at nothingness as I tried to find anything to keep me from entering that putridity of death. And just as I reached myself, I awakened. I lay there and stared up at the ceiling, trembling like the last leaf on an oak tree in the grip of a winter wind. Slowly I lifted one arm and saw it was whole and healthy. I touched this grizzled old face, felt the wrinkles and the warm skin, the bristle of my unshaven jaw. I took a deep breath, felt my chest rise and fall. When I looked around my bedroom, it was the same as always, but bright morning sun fell through the window like beams from Heaven itself."

Annie could not take her eyes off the man. She had taken that dream journey with him; she felt his desperation, and then his determination and arrogance, and—lastly—his terror.

"What … what did you do then, when you got up?"

He leaned back in his chair, relaxing for the first time since he began his tale.

"It took me a while to have the strength to rise from that bed. Maybe a couple of hours. I was weak all over; whether from leftover fear brought on by that dream or from pure relief that my death had been an illusion, I'm not sure. But as I lay there, I realized something had shifted in my mind and in my heart. The fortune I had so single-mindedly pursued and amassed had brought me to a place that no longer meant anything to me. Because I had hoarded much of my wealth, spending only on myself, I knew it would take years for me to spend it all. In fact, I was sure I would be moldering in my grave, and my money would still lie in the world's banks, helping no one. At that point, I chose to change. I would share what I had stubbornly clung to. And I hoped that—when I do die—I would not be a rotted, undiscovered corpse."

He met Annie's eyes. "It has taken me a while to realize that helping people is a far better motivation for giving than the hope your body would be found soon after death."

"My goodness," she said faintly. "What an ordeal that dream was."

"It rather echoes Ebenezer Scrooge, doesn't it? But my dream was not a story in a book; my dream happened."

She leaned forward, smiling at him. "You have made so many people happy, Graham. I look forward to watching you embrace this new life you've chosen."

His face creased with joy. "Thank you for saying so. Stony Point is only my beginning."

"I'm still curious, though," she said. "Why Stony Point, Maine? Why not some town in, say, Arizona, or Oregon, or Mississippi?"

He shrugged. "I pulled out an old map of the United States, closed my eyes, and Stony Point is where my finger landed. I flew from New York to Portland, had a cab bring me here and drop me off at the bank. All I had were the clothes on my back, that small suitcase, and some necessary paperwork. John Palmer was more than willing to work with me. And he swore to keep my secret. He, and his lovely wife."

"*Gwen?*" Annie gasped. "She knew all this time?"

"Yes, she did. She kept my secret marvelously well, don't you think? In fact, she and John have been instrumental in telling me who needed what. Gwen did the shopping for me."

"But wait a minute," Annie said slowly, "are you saying

the Palmers knew you lived in that awful old shack with inadequate heat and not enough—"

"No one knew where I lived until you snooped around and found me."

"I did not snoop!"

He chuckled. "But you did. And you found me. You— and I suppose Alice—are the only ones who know where I've been staying. Annie, do you realize how long it took me to find a place I thought no one would find? I'd been there less than a week when there you came, merrily tripping along the beach on a cold day, looking for lost souls to save while all I wanted to do was have fresh fish for my lunch."

"For someone who wanted to change from being an arrogant old so-and-so," Annie said, narrowing her eyes at him, "you certainly were hostile to me."

"Not hostile. At least I did not intend that." He reflected momentarily. "Perhaps you're right; I was hostile. It's the way I've lived most of my life. At any rate, I wanted to protect my anonymity, and you were going to ruin it by continuing to show up."

She made a little show of locking her lips and throwing away the key.

"If Gwen Palmer can tick a lock, so can Annie Dawson."

She laughed, and then a dreadful thought occurred to her.

"Noelle's clothes. Did Gwen buy them? Does she know about Noelle? What did you tell her?"

"I told her I wanted to make Christmas for a little girl who had nothing. Gwen did not ask me who; she merely bought the gifts, and I picked them up at the Palmers' house when I had dinner with them the other night. Since they live just down the road from Grey Gables, it was nothing for me to carry them this far."

"Do you think they know …?"

"About Noelle?" Graham shrugged. "Does it matter?"

"Yes! I'm not announcing her presence here just yet. I want to take care of her for a while first. She needs it so desperately. If the person who left her doesn't return for her in a reasonable amount of time, I'll have to go to child services. I've begun the process of possibly becoming her foster mother. But right now, I'm taking it one day at a time."

"Then we each have a trust in guardianship, don't we?" Graham said.

"Yes. We do," Annie replied.

"I will keep your trust. You can put your mind at rest."

"And you too."

"Good!" Graham smiled. "And now that I have spilled my proverbial guts to you, tell me about Annie Dawson, this house, and your grandparents."

He listened with great interest and had many questions about Annie's life story, which—compared to his—seemed exceedingly bland and ordinary.

Noelle came into the living room, sweetly clean in a snug little fleece suit of dark pink with pale green piping. Two green barrettes secured the sides of her hair. The sneakers on her feet seemed impossibly tiny and looked adorable. Gwen Palmer certainly knew how to shop for a little girl.

"Hello, there, young lady," Graham said.

She smiled at him shyly and sidled up to him. Then

without warning or invitation, Noelle climbed into Graham's lap. His look of astonishment was priceless, and Annie laughed aloud.

"Bambo," she said, patting his face. Then she tucked her thumb between her lips, and snuggled up to the old man's chest and sat there, perfectly content.

"Bambo?" he and Annie repeated together.

"It must be her way of saying Graham," Annie said.

"Really?"

She shrugged. "Unless maybe she thinks you're a cross between BamBam and Rambo."

Graham laughed. "I don't mind being Bambo. In fact, I rather like it."

*   *   *   *

Annie missed the next Hook and Needle Club meeting to stay with Noelle. After the meeting, Alice burst into the house via the front door, smiling and bringing cold air and a box of treats with her.

"All the ladies said to tell you 'hi' and that they missed you being there. I told them you were busy with some personal matters. And next week, I plan to have a sore throat, or maybe a sprained ankle so you can go to the meeting, and I'll stay with Noelle."

Annie looked up from where she crocheted on the sofa and nodded, smiling. She'd love nothing more than to show off Noelle to the ladies of the group.

"Thank you, Alice."

"Hey, sweetie," Alice said to Noelle where the child

sat in the old rocker, sucking her thumb sleepily. "I figured you'd be down for a nap by this time of day."

Annie paused her crocheting long enough to gaze at the sleepy girl.

"She's fighting it today for some reason. Bambo is using the treadmill in the spare room. I think she's actually fighting sleep, waiting for him to come downstairs."

"My goodness," Alice said, "by looking at the way Graham stays active, you'd never know he was eighty-five!"

"And you'd never know he has arthritis, either. He says if he keeps himself moving, he doesn't get so stiff and achy. I hope I'm that resilient when I'm his age."

"Then you should start now," he said as he joined the women. "Let me help you off with your coat, Alice. The treadmill is all yours."

"Thank you, sir! But I think you have more important matters at hand than hanging up my coat." She pointed to Noelle who had scooted off the chair and was running to him.

"Bambo!" she said, trying to climb up his leg. He reached down to lift her as easily as if she weighed less than a feather. "Hungry!" she shouted, laughing.

"Eh, you're not always so quiet, are you? And you're always hungry," he said, jostling her gently with his shoulder.

"Would you like some coffee or a cup of tea?" Annie asked the adults.

"Absolutely, some coffee would be excellent with these cookies," Alice said, holding up the box she'd brought in with her. "You'll never guess who made them, Annie."

Annie had walked toward the kitchen to start coffee, but she paused and turned.

"Not you?"

Alice shook her head. "Guess!"

"Umm, Stella?"

"Nope."

"Kate?"

Alice shook her head.

"Mary Beth?"

"No," Alice said. "OK, I'll tell you. Sara baked them! Jeff gave her permission to come before the diner opened this morning and bake them. She made scads of cookies, enough for us all to have a stash to bring home. Try one." She pried off the plastic lid and held out the box for the others to get a cookie.

"These melt in your mouth," Graham said, reaching for another.

Noelle stuffed one her mouth, grinning while she munched.

"Oh, yum!" Annie said, as she bit into the treat. "Delicious. They are crunchy and melty; they're buttery, but not too sweet or salty. Alice, you might have a competitor."

"I know! That woman can do almost anything, I believe. She made every one of those bookmarks that you took orders for, and Aaron Webster took her to Portland to deliver them. That quiet little woman was absolutely over the top because she'd made some money. And you should have seen her, Annie, wearing an outfit from all those clothes she got from Stony Point's Santa."

"What's that? I don't recall any Sara who received a gift from me," Graham said, frowning. He had cookie crumbs on his chin. Alice reached up and brushed them off.

"There is more than one Santa in this burg," she said with a merry laugh.

"There is?"

"Yes!" Annie said. "When your anonymous gifts started showing up, others began to jump on board. Someone cleaned the snow from my driveway for free—"

"And mine!" Alice chimed in. She still had no idea Annie was her Santa for that.

"Someone donated land for a community garden and others plan to donate plants and seeds, time, and labor," Annie continued. "Someone else gave Mary Beth a few items of furniture for her break room at A Stitch in Time."

The old man seemed stunned into speechlessness; then he laughed and said, "Well, let's celebrate the Christmas spirit with more cookies and some hot coffee. Or in a certain case, some milk."

"Let's do that," Alice said, "and while we're in the kitchen I have a favor I want to ask of you, Graham."

~ 21 ~

Annie put fresh water and grounds in the coffeemaker. While the coffee was brewing, she arranged Sara's cookies on a plate. She studied one, noting its pale toasty color, chunks of pecans, and something else that she could not identify. She took a bite and chewed slowly, thoughtfully, trying to assess the mysterious ingredient. Graham noticed her studious expression.

"Don't analyze. Enjoy," he said, plucking a cookie from the plate.

"Oh, I'm enjoying it immensely," Annie said, laughing, "but I love a good mystery and like to get to the bottom things."

"And she usually does," Alice said as she came into the kitchen with her purple tote bag. "Potato chips," she added, as she pulled several thick novels from the bag.

"I think there are some in the cabinet," Annie said. "You want a sandwich to go with them? I have some—"

"I didn't mean that. I meant, potato chips are the ingredient you don't recognize in the cookies. Crushed potato chips. And Sara said if you put the cookies in the freezer and eat them frozen, they are ever so good."

Annie studied the cookie with an educated eye.

"That's what gives them that extra crunch and flavor, isn't it?" she said. She enjoyed every morsel of the treat, and then she poured a small glass of milk and put one cookie on a napkin in front of Noelle. "You may have another after your nap," she promised.

Graham got three cups from the cabinet and filled them. Steam rose from each cup, lending warmth and the fragrance of coffee to the room.

"I see you've brought in some of my later novels," he said to Alice as he handed her a cup and took his usual place at the table.

"These are mine," she said, smiling. "I'd love for you to sign them for me." With a flourish, she handed him a pen. "Please?"

"It would be my honor and my delight, ma'am," he said, smiling at her. He looked at the pen with interest. "This is the first fountain pen I've seen in many years. I was unaware they still made them."

"That is the one that Charlie and Betsy gave to me as my high school graduation gift. I still use it, but only for special occasions."

"Ah. Then this is more than an honor and delight. It's a privilege."

The two women watched as he signed the flyleaf of every book, each time writing a special note to Alice.

Noelle drained the last of her milk and swallowed every cookie crumb in front of her. She rubbed her eyes, and Annie recognized the signs. If the child wasn't put down for a nap soon, she'd grow cranky and fretful.

"I'll take her for her nap," Annie said, scooping Noelle into her arms. When she returned, Graham was scowling darkly at Alice in a way Annie hadn't seen in the two weeks since he'd arrived.

"What goes on?" Annie asked cautiously. In fact, she was pretty sure she preferred not to know.

"I was telling Graham I thought it would be grand to have an autograph party. We could advertise it in *The Point*, announce it on the radio—"

"Absolutely not! I refuse to be made a laughing-stock, pointed out as a pathetic has-been writer who is *irrelevant*."

"But this might re-launch your career—"

"No!" he all but roared. "That's it, Alice. No!"

The two women exchanged glances. Annie silently signaled for her friend to drop the subject.

"I understand how you feel, Graham," Annie said, "and certainly you don't have to do such a thing. But I've been thinking about what you said, about critics saying you were irrelevant."

Something glittered in his eyes and before he grew more upset, she rushed to continue.

"They did not say *you* were irrelevant. They said your last book was. And you know why? Because it was about the Cold War."

"But that's my area of expertise! That's the subject I built my career on."

"But, Graham, maybe you've said all that needs to be said about that time. Maybe readers don't want to read about it because they know how it ends. Whatever the critics say, it's not you or your writing—it's the subject. You just need to find a new topic."

"Bah!" he said, moving restlessly in his chair.

"I have a point, if you'll just be patient with me," Annie said. "You talked about how you've changed—and why. You described that dream you had, and I found myself so caught up in it all. I felt what you felt, way down deep inside myself. And I know I'm not the only one who would feel that way. Graham, that's a story that *is* relevant. I think *that's* the story you should write."

"And bare that part of my soul to the world? Never!"

"But isn't that what writing ultimately is? Baring a part of your soul to the world? By doing so you may be able to erase or alleviate someone else's painful search. You could help them by sharing how your single-minded search for wealth and fame took you outside the human experience and left you feeling alone and irrelevant?"

"Yes!" Alice said. "Although I missed the story of all that you went through, Graham, if you were to record the differences you've made in the lives of others by your anonymous gifts, you'd bring so much joy to others."

"And by sharing how," Annie added, "at the advanced age of eighty-five, you were able to put aside a lifetime of misguided thinking, you can give so much hope." She saw his resistance begin to weaken.

"Don't you want to write again?" she asked quietly.

"I love the art and the craft of writing fiction," he admitted slowly.

"Will you think about it?" Alice asked.

He hesitated a moment longer, and then a spark flickered in his sea-gray eyes.

"I will," he promised, "but only as a novel, not as a glorified autobiography."

~ 22 ~

he fire roared in the fireplace, and the Christmas tree shimmered in reflection of the flames. From the kitchen wafted the scent of cinnamon, pumpkin, sage, ham ... almost every delectable Christmas food that American tradition could call for.

Carols played softly on the CD player tucked unobtrusively behind the tree. On the rococo table, Annie had placed some fresh, fragrant cedar branches around one of Gram's favorite nativity scenes, with tiny porcelain figures as delicate as spiderwebs. Noelle had been firmly instructed that this one display must never be touched by little hands. For the entire week that it had been on display, she had stood with her hands clasped behind her back, her pale eyes gazing with wonder at the scene depicting the first Christmas night.

In the weeks since Noelle's arrival, she had filled out. Thin cheeks were beginning to take on a childish roundness. Her arms and legs looked less and less like fragile thin sticks and more like a toddler's sturdy limbs. The clothes Annie and Graham had bought now fit without being pinned. Noelle wore a red velvet dress with a full skirt and lace-trimmed collar and puffed sleeves. The black velvet sash around her waist was tied in a huge bow in the back. Lacy white anklets and shiny black patent-leather Mary Janes completed the child's outfit and contrasted sweetly with her silvery-blond hair and sparkly red barrettes. She was hunkered in front of the Christmas tree, staring at her many reflections in the multicolored glass balls. From time to time, a tentative fingertip reached out to touch the ball, and she jumped in place a little, giggling. She ignored the gifts. No doubt presents had been few and far between in her life, if she had received any at all. Her pale eyes now shone with an inner light, and fear seemed a distant memory for the little girl.

Four doting adults watched her and chatted as they sipped mulled cider and munched the plethora of Christmas treats Annie and Alice had prepared.

"Ladies, the fragrance from that dinner is wending its way into my heart not to mention my olfactory passages," Ian said from his place next to Annie on the sofa. He wore a dark red-and-green long-sleeve tartan shirt and black slacks. Annie's deep green sweater sported a feathery faux-fur collar and looked lovely with her black velvet slacks. In her hair, she had fastened a sparkling angel hairpin that had belonged to Betsy. Sitting next to Ian, she had to admit they complemented each other quite well, right down to their polished leather shoes. Maybe they *were* an item.

"It's almost ready," Alice said. "The rolls are baking, and once I take them from the oven, it will be time to feast." She looked lovely in her black turtleneck and red vest. She had embroidered glossy, dark green holly leaves and gold berries along the neckline. Her red slacks matched the color of the vest exactly. With her furnace repaired—she said she hoped it was repaired for *good* this time—Alice had moved back to the carriage house.

They were having dinner on Christmas Eve at Grey Gables because the next day Graham would be having dinner with the Palmers.

"You must come too, Annie," Gwen had said when she found out that Graham was staying with her.

"Thank you, Gwen, that's so sweet of you, but I'm afraid I already have plans," Annie had replied. Those plans entailed staying home, sharing the day with Ian, Alice, and Noelle, and that suited Annie just fine.

"I do believe I will need to buy myself a new wardrobe soon," Graham declared. "Your fine cooking has laid waste to my waist."

"Ohhh," Alice groaned at the joke. She eyed his red wool sweater and dark brown corduroy pants. "Well, you have a long way to go, Graham Cartwright, and if you happen to reach that point in the next week or so, that's what all those diet programs are for. You know—the ones that fill the TV airwaves on the second day of January."

Ian grinned at the man he'd met only a few days earlier. It had taken persistent wheedling from Annie before Graham agreed to meet the town's mayor. But the two had hit it off immediately and talked in depth about the town and how much Graham's help had meant. They also talked about books; Ian was fascinated by the whole experience of crafting a story from beginning to end.

At that moment, it seemed they all had been lifelong friends, and Annie was grateful for that. Although it was Christmas Eve, and she still missed LeeAnn, Herb, and the twins terribly, she felt content that night, surrounded by such warmth and friendship. A niggling unease reminded her that as much as she loved the little girl, Noelle was not hers and probably would leave someday.

I refuse to think about that tonight, she told herself firmly. *I'm going to embrace this Christmas with a joyful heart and store up blessed memories.*

Noelle jumped up from where she'd been gazing into the ornaments and ran to the nativity scene. From there she skipped over to the fireplace and stood still while the firelight played across her fair skin and pale hair. She turned to Annie with an impish grin.

"Hungry!" she announced.

"We'll be eating soon," Annie told her.

"I'll see how the rolls are coming," Alice said. "Stay right there, Annie, and relax. I got this."

Alice came into the living room a few minutes later and said, "My friends, dinner is served."

"Yay!" Noelle shouted, clapping. She rushed into the dining room and clambered into her new high chair, a gift from Graham. Special order and rushed to be delivered that day, it was adjustable to fit the table as she grew. Noelle had danced around the chair when it was pulled from the packing material.

They had just taken their seats, and Ian had asked the blessing on the meal, when someone knocked on the front door.

"Goodness," Annie said, getting up. "Who in the world could that be? Excuse me, please."

She turned on the porch light and opened her front door. Sara Downs stood there, an uncertain smile on her face.

"Why, Sara!" Annie said. "Come in out of the cold."

The woman ducked her head and stepped inside. Wondering why Sara had come calling unexpectedly on Christmas Eve, Annie closed the door against the cold night and turned a smile to her visitor. Sara was dressed in the new coat Annie and Alice had bought, and she had curled her lank hair. A touch of lipstick, a bit of blusher and mascara, and a brush of eye shadow gave her a younger, healthier appearance.

"We're just getting ready to have dinner," Annie said. "Would you like to join us?"

"No, thank you. I'm so sorry to drop in on you this way, Annie, but I think it's time I—"

There was a shriek and a crash in the dining room.

"Nanny!" Noelle screamed.

"Oh, my goodness," Annie said, running toward the room. Noelle flew past her, screeching, "Nanny, Nanny!!"

"Oh, Baby Girl!" Sara said, catching up the child as Noelle leapt into her arms. She smothered the little face with kisses. "Happy birthday and merry Christmas! Nanny has missed you *so much*!"

Annie stood, rooted the spot, stunned into silence. The others came out of the dining room and stood in a cluster, all of them staring at Noelle and Sara. No one said a word.

Sara turned to Annie, tears swimming in her eyes.

"Thank you for taking care of Noelle. I knew you had a mother's heart and a grandmother's love; I knew she'd come to no harm with you."

Somehow Annie found her voice.

"Sara, I don't understand. Who is she? Is she your daughter?"

"Noelle is my granddaughter."

"How ... I mean, why ... oh Sara, what happened?"

The other woman was chalk white beneath her make-up. Her hazel eyes were wide and frightened, but she clung tightly to Noelle.

"I had to do something!" she said fiercely. "I had to make sure Noelle was taken care of."

Something inside Annie made her want to run away from whatever Sara was going to say, but she knew she had to hear it. This was the moment Annie had dreaded for weeks, but now she had to be strong.

Annie put her arm around the woman's shoulders and said, "Why don't you take off your coat, and let's go into the living room where we can talk." She looked at the others. "Please go on with your dinner."

"Annie?" Alice said, her eyes filled with concern.

"It's all right," Annie assured her.

"Come," Ian said, guiding Graham and Alice back into the dining room. Sara juggled Noelle from one arm to the other while she removed her coat and then settled on the sofa with the child in her lap.

"She looks so sweet," Sara said, running her hands along the velvet dress and then stroking Noelle's hair. "And healthy. Annie, you've taken real good care of her, and I'm ever so thankful."

"I was happy to take care of Noelle. She's a sweet little girl," Annie said softly, "but, Sara, I deserve an explanation."

"Yes, you do," Sara agreed, "and that's why I'm here. I'm awfully sorry I've put you through all this, but you see, a couple of weeks ago my daughter showed up at the

Atlantic Jewel and left Noelle with me. She gave me no explanation other than she had other things to do, and Noelle was in her way. I've been providing for the two of them as best I could since Noelle's birth—which was three years ago today—but several months ago, Pamela decided she didn't need or want me. She took off for parts unknown, but not before she'd raised such a ruckus at my workplace that I got fired. And of course, no job means no food and no place to live. I could've got a cook's job in Portland, but I wanted to go somewhere quiet, somewhere I could think about my life and make some changes—maybe put down some roots." She seemed to wilt. "I figured I'd never see my daughter or granddaughter again, and I had to start picking up the pieces of my own life."

"And you chose Stony Point."

She nodded. "I'd heard about the town, and how the local crafting club did things for the community. I was ever so glad I met Peggy at The Cup & Saucer after I moved here. People were so nice to me—Jeff, Peggy, and you. And Mr. Webster, of course—he's been real sweet and real patient with me about my rent."

"He's a kind man, I'm sure. But Sara, why did you leave Noelle at Grey Gables? I mean, you just abandoned her here, with no one home and the windows open."

Sara lifted tortured eyes to Annie. She reached out and wrapped her cold, trembling fingers around one of Annie's hands, as if clutching it could make Annie understand.

"One afternoon shortly after I got off work, Pamela showed up at my door. I don't know how she tracked me down, and she didn't say. She just knocked on my door, handed over Noelle, her little bear and the pink blanket, and told me to keep her. I tried to talk some sense into her, but all she did was scream at me, get in a beat-up old car with some rough-looking fellow, and they sped away like the law was after them. Maybe it was; I don't know."

Sara pulled Noelle even closer and continued. "Mr. Webster is a great manager, but he's not the owner, and he can't change the rules. No kids are allowed at the Atlantic Jewel. If I kept Noelle, we'd have had to live on the street because I don't even have a car."

Sara shrugged helplessly. "All I knew was that I had to make sure Noelle was safe and warm and well-fed. She couldn't live with me, and I had no money to move anywhere else. Taking her to work with me was out of the question. That kitchen is no place for a little girl, even if Jeff would allow it. Annie, I was desperate, and then I remembered you said at the meeting that you'd left your windows open because of the burnt popcorn smell. I found Grey Gables, and I had little trouble getting inside. The best I could do was bundle up Noelle, give her something she could eat easily, and leave her. I *knew* you'd keep her safe for me. You're that kind of woman."

"But, Sara, all you had to do was ask me. I would have been happy to let you and Noelle stay in Grey Gables while you got on your feet."

The woman gave her a wretched look. "You were missing your grandkids so much, I thought—I *prayed*—that Noelle would be a blessing to you. But don't you see, I didn't want to burden you with me too."

Annie took this in, and prayed silently that she could

respond from a pure heart. "She *has* been a blessing, Sara," she said, gripping the woman's cold fingers in her own. "These last few weeks have been pure joy. I thank you for that. But you know something? *You* would have been a welcome blessing too, because you're a sweet, caring person. I'm proud to call you my friend."

At this, Sara's eyes filled again, and she began to sob. Noelle saw her grandmother's tears and began to cry too. Annie joined them, a trio of weeping females, fulfilling the needs of one another in a way none had fully realized.

"Annie," Sara said, "please forgive me for making such an awful mistake. I was ... I was just so ...."

"Desperate," Annie supplied. "But, Sara, believe me when I say the biggest mistake you made was not asking me, and for that, I forgive you."

Sara swallowed hard, mascara tracking down her thin cheeks. "Thank you," she whispered. "Thank you so much!"

"You're so welcome," Annie said with a tear-stained smile. "And now, there is one thing you must do to make up for all this."

Sara nodded. "If I can."

"Move in to Grey Gables until you're on your feet."

She watched as it seemed a thousand pounds had lifted from the small shoulders.

"Oh, Annie. Really?"

"Really."

"It shouldn't be long. The people at Books Galore and The Gift Gallery want me to make bookmarks and other specialty items for every holiday," Sara said. "With what I earn at The Cup & Saucer, and with what they will pay me for

my crocheted work, I'll be able to support Noelle and myself
soon. But until then ... are you sure about me being here?"

"I'm sure. I love having a full house." Annie stood up
and gently drew Sara to her feet, turning her and Noelle toward the dining room. "Come with me. We're having a family
dinner, and there is always room for one more at my table."

Annie handed Sara a box of tissues so she could wipe
away little Noelle's tears and her own. When they were all
presentable again, the three joined Ian, Alice, and Graham
at the dining room table.

Annie glanced across the room at Graham, who was
beaming at Sara and Noelle as the small group encircled the
table for a delectable Christmas Eve meal. Annie suspected
that Noelle and her grandmother might be the recipients
of one more substantial Christmas gift from Stony Point's
Santa. But the best gift Noelle could ever receive was the
unconditional love that Sara wrapped her in that night.

Annie had known all along that Noelle would one day
leave her life as quickly as she had come into it. At least
that day was pushed back for a while longer. Things would
get back to normal, and Annie would plan a trip soon to see
LeeAnn, Herb, John and Joanna. But she also knew that this
Christmas—the Christmas that began with such desperation
and loneliness—would always have a special place in her
heart. How could Annie ever forget the little gift she found
at Grey Gables? She would be reminded every year as she
joined with others to sing the words to that ancient carol:

Noel! Noel!
Noel! Noel!
Born is the King of Israel!